"Run, Erin!" Amelia screamed. "The tree's coming down!"

I ran crouched over, so scared that I couldn't even yell. And the instant I reached the end of the bridge, the tree fell. I leaped forward and fell on the land. Then I looked back and saw the bridge disappear under water. Pain shot across my lower back and down my left leg.

"You're hurt," Amelia said.

"Not really. I'll be okay in a minute."

"So what do we do now?" Heather asked. "How do we get off this island?"

White-hot pain shot down my left leg, from my back to my heel. The day went on and on. My cousins invented a dozen plans to get us off the island, but none of them were workable.

I think we were all half-asleep when I heard the sound first.

"Listen!" I said. "Toby's here."

It was nearly dark. Amelia helped me sit up as I heard the paddle in the lake. The pain in my back was like a wild thing biting me, and I hated having him see me like this.

He knelt beside me. "Hey," he said. "I know you didn't like the bridge, but did you have to knock it down?"

In spite of everything, I laughed, and without thinking, reached out to him.

He wrapped his arms around me and whispered, "I'll take you home."

Don't Miss the Other Adventures of
THE WHITNEY COUSINS

AMELIA
ERIN
HEATHER

. . . and **THE BIRTHDAY GIRLS**

WHO AM I, ANYWAY?
MIRROR, MIRROR
I'M NOT TELLING

Other Avon Flare Books

APPOINTMENT WITH A STRANGER
COULDN'T I START OVER?
THE LAST APRIL DANCERS
WAS IT SOMETHING I SAID?
WHEN DOES THE FUN START?
WHO SAID LIFE IS FAIR?

THE WHITNEY COUSINS

TRIPLE TROUBLE

JEAN THESMAN

AN AVON  FLARE BOOK

THE WHITNEY COUSINS: TRIPLE TROUBLE is an original publication of Avon Books. This work has never before appeared in book form. This work is a novel. Any similarity to actual persons or events is purely coincidental.

AVON BOOKS
A division of
The Hearst Corporation
1350 Avenue of the Americas
New York, New York 10019

Copyright © 1992 by Jean Thesman
Published by arrangement with the author
Library of Congress Catalog Card Number: 92-93065
ISBN: 0-380-76464-4
RL: 5.2

First Avon Flare Printing: September 1992

AVON FLARE TRADEMARK REG. U.S. PAT. OFF. AND IN OTHER COUNTRIES, MARCA REGISTRADA, HECHO EN U.S.A.

Printed in the U.S.A.

RA   10   9   8   7   6   5   4   3   2   1

Chapter 1

Dear Nick: It takes an hour and five minutes to walk from one side of Fox Crossing to the other. I'll never last in this town until the end of August. Help!

Erin (City Girl) Whitney

I'd been in Fox Crossing with my cousin, Heather, for not quite twenty-four hours when I wrote that desperate letter to my pal, Nicholas Brown. My other cousin, Amelia, the one I lived with in Seattle, was visiting Heather, too. Amelia was crazy about the idea of staying several weeks in that neat and tidy little town. But she was a typical fifteen-year-old, like Heather, and I knew for certain that they'd spend the rest of the summer giggling about boyfriends and clothes, and you can do that anywhere.

I was fifteen, too, but boyfriends and clothes seemed like kid stuff. (Well, clothes were kid stuff. I knew a boy in Seattle that I liked, but I didn't talk much about him.)

Don't get me wrong. I loved my cousins, but about the only thing we had in common was our bright green eyes. And I also loved Seattle and my friends there, especially good old Nick. Even though he was only fourteen, he was a college student taking summer classes. Earlier that summer I'd been on campus, too, enrolled in a special art course for high school students.

But now the course was over. Aunt Ellen and Uncle Jock, who were Amelia's parents and my guardians, decided to head for Oklahoma for Aunt Ellen's family reunion. Uncle Jock had saved his vacation time for two years for this. Amelia and I were given the choice of going along in the van with them (and my little cousins Jamie, age 10; Cassie, age 6; and Mimi, age 5) or spending the summer in Fox Crossing with Heather, her mother, and her new stepfather.

"I would rather die than be stuck in the van with the little guys for weeks and weeks and weeks," Amelia had said when we heard the news. "They argue and whine and get crumbs all over everybody."

"Who wants to be stuck with *you* anywhere?" Jamie had demanded, outraged.

"Amelia, you've got to come to Oklahoma with us!" Cassie had wept. Her idea of paradise was having the entire family in one room forever.

"*I* always want to go to Fox Crossing!" shouted Mimi, who didn't even know where Fox Crossing was.

We'd had this quiet (ha ha) family discussion at the dinner table, and before the meal was over, everybody's plans were set. Aunt Ellen, Uncle Jock, and the little guys would drive to Oklahoma; Amelia and I would take the bus to Fox Crossing, in northern Washington State; and the family dogs would move in with Mark Reid, Amelia's boyfriend.

Later that evening, after I'd walked over to Nick's house to give him the news, he peered earnestly at me through his glasses and advised me to reconsider my plans.

"You can stay here with my family," he said. "We can hang out on the campus together."

2

I laughed. "Yeah, I remember how you hang out there. You feed the squirrels and watch the real college kids hang out."

Nick yanked my long braid a little harder than he usually did. "They'll get used to me and the other kids in the special classes. They have to. We're going to be there for years. And we're not the only short people on the campus."

"Short," I scoffed. "Short isn't the problem. But I think that maybe you kids are holding your own. I could tell that whenever I saw you running across campus between classes. You were all brains and business, even though your lunch boxes did have cartoon characters on them."

"Whereas you guys in the art program were lying around under the trees talking about perspective and negative space and the real meaning of the color blue," Nick said disrespectfully.

I rubbed my knuckles hard on his scalp. "I'm going to miss you between now and the end of August, you little twerp," I said. "There won't be anybody like you in Fox Crossing."

"There won't be anybody like Brady Harris, either," he said, leering.

"Shut up about him," I said. I'd already phoned Brady and told him about Fox Crossing. As soon as I left Nick's, I was heading for Brady's. We'd go for a ride and talk. In a few more days, we'd be saying good-bye for weeks. Too many weeks. I wasn't exactly sure whether or not he was my boyfriend, but he was pretty close to it. Pretty close for me, at least. I didn't make friends easily. And after my parents died when I was ten, I never wanted to feel as if I couldn't get along without certain people. It just wasn't safe.

* * *

So Amelia and I traveled to Fox Crossing on the bus and moved in with Heather, in a big, beautiful house a few blocks from the college where Dr. Will Carver, her stepfather, taught.

Heather had a stepsister, too, but Tracey had gone to England for the summer with her boyfriend's family, so Amelia and I moved into Tracey's room and unpacked.

We were watched carefully by Heather's enormous black dog, Bear.

"I can't decide if that dog likes me or hates me," I told Amelia.

"Bear likes everybody," Heather said from the doorway. "But Thad—he's the boy who gave Bear to me—Thad taught her to wait until you call her before she comes up to you. She's sorta big and—"

"Big doesn't describe her," I said, eyeing Bear. "She looks like she's part buffalo." I snapped my fingers and called out to the dog.

She leaped toward me, a great, furry lump, and nearly knocked me down. I wasn't in doubt any longer. Bear liked me. A lot.

The next morning after breakfast, Heather took Amelia and me for a walk around Fox Crossing. It wasn't even ten o'clock yet, but I was glad that I was wearing shorts and a thin blouse, because the July sun was hot. In the distance, the mountains seemed to shimmer against the horizon.

In the gorgeous, big park across the street from the college, we met two of Heather's friends, Paige Worth—who looked so much like Heather that it was eerie—and Micky Logan, a cute, dark-haired girl.

"How's the work on the Centennial coming along?" Micky asked Heather.

Heather groaned and dropped down on a park

4

bench. "Don't ask. I'm up to my ears in envelopes and stamps."

"This has something to do with the hundred-year celebration for the college?" Amelia asked, as she sat on the grass at Heather's feet.

"You heard about it?" Heather asked.

"Your mom told my mom something about it," Amelia said.

"Sure, I remember," I said to Heather, making an effort to be a part of things. I was learning to be a little friendlier than I had once been. "Your stepfather is heading up the committee that's planning the celebration."

"And I volunteered to help out," Heather said. "But I had no idea what I was getting into."

"We can all help," Micky said. "At least, I can for the next few days. Then I leave for the ocean. I wish you could come, Heather."

Heather shook her head. "I can't. As soon as I finish the mailings, I know Will's going to need me to do something else, and then something else after that. And I can't let him down. With Tracey gone, he's depending on me."

"Heather, were you going to the ocean?" Amelia asked quickly. "Did we come at the wrong time?"

"There is no wrong time," Heather said. "I wouldn't have given up having you here, not for anything."

"Gee," Amelia said, "you should have told us that you had plans. We could have gone to Oklahoma."

"I didn't have plans!" Heather cried, and now she sounded exasperated. "Honestly! I knew it would be impossible to go to the ocean with Micky's family."

"We'll only be gone a couple of weeks," Micky explained quickly.

"Two weeks doesn't sound long," Amelia said.

5

"Why don't you go, Heather? Whatever you'd do for Uncle Will, I can do. And Erin will help."

Ha. I didn't remember volunteering, but I guess, if you're part of a family, you help out whenever you're needed.

But Heather had made up her mind that she couldn't go, no matter for how short a time. "Will's counting on me," she said. "The committee can't afford too many salaried people, and I'm taking the place of a secretary."

"You're typing?" Paige asked incredulously. "I don't believe it. You barely passed typing class. You were the one who never noticed when your hands were on the wrong part of the keyboard."

"Don't remind me," Heather said. "If it weren't for the correction key on Will's typewriter, I'd still be working on the first letter. But he doesn't complain. And this is giving me a chance to get to know him better. After all, I haven't even lived here for a year yet."

"Some year," Paige snickered. "It's been a lifetime for some people in Fox Crossing."

I'd heard about the mischief they made in school, and remembering it, I grinned. Together, they'd driven their vice principal half-crazy, and I couldn't think of a more satisfying hobby.

Just then a tall, dark-haired man strode along the path toward the white building south of us that Heather had pointed out as the City Hall.

"Good morning, Mr. Callahan," Heather said when he leveled a cold glance at her. She sounded nervous.

He didn't answer her, but strode along as if she hadn't said anything to him. Or maybe as if she wasn't worth the bother of a reply.

6

"That's the may.... of earshot.

"Big jerk," Paige mum....

"What's wrong with him?....

"He doesn't like Will," Heath.... really. Will can get along with anyb.... world, but Mr. Callahan goes out of h.... rude. Will was picked by the college to hea.... committee for the Centennial, and Mr. Callahan.... .s mad because he wanted to do it, even though he doesn't have anything to do with the college."

"It's because his great-grandfather was one of the college founders," Paige supplied. "He thinks he ought to run the entire world because of that."

"So he's rude to Will and me and everybody else on the committee whenever he sees us," Heather said.

Grown-ups, I thought. They act more like kids than kids do.

We didn't stay in the park very long after that, because Heather had to finish addressing envelopes for Uncle Will. As soon as we got back to the house, she disappeared inside the den, and moments later we heard the typewriter clicking again.

Aunt Marsha, Heather's mother, worked as a volunteer at a free medical clinic on the other side of town, so Amelia and I were left on our own for a while. She found a book that appealed to her in one of the living room bookcases, and I wrote my letter to Nicholas. Then I took my sketchbook and pencils outside.

Bear accompanied me. She watched me earnestly, her head cocked to one side. She was so appealing that I ended up making several sketches of her, and she seemed to understand and approve of what I was doing.

"You're weird," I told her.

a dog! And she deserved a reward. I
inside, put on one of my large collection of
weird, secondhand hats (white straw, pink roses, only
slightly squashed), and took the leash I'd seen off the
hook inside the door. As soon as I got out on the
porch with it, Bear went slightly mad, leaping about
and barking.

Heather stuck her head out the door. "Good grief,"
she said. "You aren't seriously volunteering to take
that moose for a walk."

"Why not?" I asked.

Heather laughed. "Bear has a favorite route," she
said. "You'll find that you can't walk her anywhere
else."

"So I'll go where she wants to go," I said as I
fastened the leash to Bear's collar. "Which direction?"

"North," Heather said, and she grinned. "Good
luck."

I didn't take Bear for a walk. She took me. We
certainly did go north, blocks and blocks north. She
did allow me to drop my letter into a mailbox, but
she clearly didn't want me to dawdle.

"Do you have to *run?*" I asked.

She didn't bother answering. She led me to a big
house and straight up on the porch, and she scratched
on the door as if she'd been there a hundred times.

A tall, nice-looking boy opened the door.

"Well, Bear," he said. "I see you've brought Erin
over for a visit."

Another dog, one that looked a lot like Bear, burst
out the door and cavorted around Bear.

"That's Heidi," the boy said. "And I'm Thad.
Heather phoned and said that you'd be showing up
here pretty soon."

Heather hadn't been joking when she said that Bear knew where she wanted to go. I said, "I take it that these two dogs are related?"

"Sisters. They go for walks together nearly every day. But I've got to run an errand in a couple of minutes, so I can't take Heidi out now. You've got your work cut out if you're going to haul Bear off the porch without her sister."

I looked down at Bear and knew he was telling the truth.

"So now what?" I asked.

Another boy appeared behind him and said, "Is there something I can do?"

Thad laughed. "When I shut the door, pull Bear off the porch and get her started home with Erin. She won't want to go."

He wasn't kidding. Bear bellowed while he dragged Heidi inside and closed the door. The other boy, who was much taller than Thad, had trouble hauling Bear down the steps, even with me behind shoving her as hard as I could.

"This dog doesn't know much about obedience," the boy said. But he was grinning.

He had wonderful eyes, golden, flecked with green, and a bit slanted. His hair was black and a little too long, and it fell over his tanned forehead. He grinned and then looked away, as if he regretted being so friendly to a complete stranger.

"Bear doesn't need to know much about obedience," I said. "I bet she does as she pleases most of the time." My mouth was dry and my voice shook a little. What was wrong with me? I was always the coolest girl around.

"Do you think you can manage the dog now?" he asked, as he handed the leash back to me. "She's enormous, and you're not very big. The two of you look like a bug taking an elephant for a walk."

Bear sighed lustily and plodded away from the house, head down. Her day had been ruined.

"Obviously she's giving up the fight," I called back over my shoulder.

"Great," the boy said, and he bounded back up the steps.

"Hey," he said, with a heartbreaking grin. "I love your hat."

Then without another word, he let himself inside the house.

My mind was a perfect blank.

Chapter 2

Dear Nick: Thanks for calling to cheer me up, but it's hopeless. Believe it or not, I'm really going to a *barn dance* near a place called Abbey Falls! Heather and her friends say we'll meet lots of nice country boys. I don't get much attention at dances in the city. Can you picture me waiting all night for a guy with his knuckles dragging on the ground to say, "Yo, babe, wanna dance?"

> Laugh and I'll kill you,
> Erin

My first week in Fox Crossing wasn't too bad, but I missed Seattle and Nick—and Brady Harris, too. Amelia didn't say much, but I knew she was lonely for Mark. But then, they were a real couple, not just good pals like Brady and me.

That's all we were, I thought. Pals. Neither of us had ever been big on romantic declarations or commitments meant to last until the end of time. He'd helped me when I needed it, and I wasn't about to forget it. And I'd sure never turned him down when he invited me to go to a movie with him. But I wasn't certain of anything else.

Aunt Ellen and Uncle Jock phoned us every third night to report on their trip to Oklahoma. After hearing about the flat tire, the leak in the gas tank, Mimi throwing up in the roadside diner, and Jamie getting lost in a theme park, Amelia and I congratulated each other on being smart enough to pick Fox Crossing for our vacation.

But, then again, there wasn't a whole lot to do.

"We could walk around the campus again," Amelia suggested one morning when we were trying to decide how to spend another hot July day.

She and I were still sitting at the kitchen table, sharing the last of the breakfast orange juice. Down the hall, Heather was tap-tapping on the typewriter in the den, while Uncle Will murmured into the telephone to somebody about providing a bandstand and bleachers for the Centennial celebration. Aunt Marsha was sewing a button on her nurse's uniform and scowling. Her feet rested on Bear, who was sound asleep.

"We could go to the library," I told Amelia. We'd been there the day before, but I like libraries.

"Both of you could plan what you're going to wear to the dance tonight," Heather called out from the den.

Hmm, I thought. What does a girl wear to a barn dance? I didn't know if this would be one of those folk-dancing affairs that I'd seen on TV, where the girls wore full skirts over stiff petticoats, or jeans and plaid shirts. And I wasn't too keen on either idea.

"What are you going to wear?" I called back to Heather.

Silence. Finally she said, "Well, maybe I'll wear the same dress I wore the other night when we went to the movie. Doesn't that sound all right?"

It had been an ordinary summer dress, and Amelia had brought one that was somewhat like it. But I, of course, an expert on absolutely ridiculous clothes, didn't have anything with that nice, crisp, cottony look.

"Will it be all right if I wear my long striped skirt and a yellow shirt?" I asked Amelia, who was watching me and grinning. My weird taste in clothes struck her as funny. Most of the time, anyway.

"Perfect," Amelia said. Tap-tap went Heather's typewriter in the other room. "Or you could borrow something of mine," Amelia added.

"I'll stick with the long skirt," I said.

My aunt looked up at me over the top of her reading glasses. "I like your clothes, Erin. You remind me of one of those old-fashioned dolls. Long hair, long skirts, hats. All you need is a parasol."

"Romantic," Amelia said, sighing. "A parasol with lace on the edge. Brady would love it."

I didn't say anything. My mind was suddenly paralyzed, because I'd remembered the boy I'd met at Thad Shipton's when Bear took me there for a walk.

I didn't even know his name! I was being completely ridiculous.

"Let's do up the breakfast dishes," I said to Amelia, and I jumped to my feet.

"You're a darling girl and I'm planning on keeping you forever," Aunt Marsha said. She grinned at me as she carried her uniform out of the room. "I'm leaving in ten minutes. Does anyone need a ride anywhere?"

Nobody needed a ride. Uncle Will finished his conversation and phoned somebody else. Bear yawned hugely and eyed me with momentary hope.

"No walk today," I said.

She let her head drop to the floor with a thud and fell immediately back to sleep.

I started clearing the kitchen table. "Shall we go to the library or the campus?" I asked Amelia.

"You could go to the printer's with me!" Heather

13

called out. "I'm picking up the posters today. I could use some help."

"We can put them up for you," Amelia offered.

"Not today." Heather appeared in the kitchen doorway, ink smudged on her chin. "Will doesn't want them to go up until next week. That way people won't be too tired of looking at them by the time the Centennial starts." She hugged herself suddenly. "Just think. It's only a few weeks away. There'll be hundreds of people here who graduated from the college. Already most of the dormitory rooms have been reserved. We're having the biggest dinner the town's ever seen. And fireworks. And music and all sorts of stuff."

Now that sounded interesting. I stopped scraping plates and pushed back my hair. "You ought to get Amelia to put on a clown act for you," I said. "She's really good."

"I can't do it alone," Amelia said, "and there's no way I could persuade the whole troupe to come here."

Heather looked at her in a strange way. "But you could teach other kids to do some of the stuff, couldn't you? I mean, you could teach Paige—she's terrific with costumes and stuff like that, and she has a great sense of humor. Would you try?"

Amelia looked doubtful. "I don't know. It's not as easy as it sounds."

"Well, Erin could help. She's seen you do your clown act a hundred times, I bet."

"No way," I said. "Forget that. I'll help, if I can, in some other way. I can letter signs and banners and posters, if that's any help . . ."

"You bet it is!" Heather said. "You're on!"

But she wasn't done with Amelia yet. "Come on, cousin. Work up a clown act for us. We've got several

14

performers for that day—musicians and some dancers—but we can always use more, especially something really good."

Amelia didn't look too happy about the idea, but
she agreed to try, if she could find other people to
help out, people who were good athletes or dancers.
Clowning around was hard work.

"I'll know lots of kids at the dance tonight,"
Heather said. "You just wait. I'll find plenty of help
for you."

Amelia was wearing a panicky expression, but
Heather didn't notice. I went back to the dishes, glad
I didn't have Amelia's job. I know how hard she and
the clown troupe worked to perfect every act. She
wouldn't have much time—especially since she'd be
working with beginners.

The day grew hotter, but later on in the afternoon,
dark clouds gathered on the horizon, and Uncle Will
told us that we'd have a thunderstorm before the next
morning.

"You kids drive with extra care if the rain should
start before you get home tonight," he warned us.

My cousins and I were dressed and waiting for
Thad, who was driving us to Abbey Falls. Heather
and Amelia looked wonderful in their summer
dresses. I suspected that I looked like somebody's
grandmother, but I didn't care. Not much, at any rate.
Only when I thought of that strange boy at Thad's the
other day and I wondered if he'd be going with us.

Thad arrived alone. I hated myself for being disappointed. After all, I had Brady back in Seattle. And
nobody ever really develops an interest in somebody
the first time she sees him. Not really. Not in real
life. Not a girl like Erin Whitney, the most eccentric
orphan around.

15

Nick would die laughing if he knew what I was thinking.

Or rather, what I was trying not to think.

Who was that boy? He had such strange eyes. Clear and quiet. I thought of green and gold leaves glimmering on the bottom of a crystal pond.

"Hey, wake up," Amelia said.

I blinked and looked around. Everybody was waiting at the door for me.

"Enjoy yourselves," Uncle Will said as we left.

I could smell rain in the air, and the branches on the trees tossed angrily over us. I shivered a little as we climbed into Thad's car, buckled up, and left.

It took half an hour to reach Abbey Falls. The barn dance wasn't actually being held in a barn—it was set up in the community center. The dancing had already begun when we arrived, and it wasn't square dancing, either.

I was almost disappointed. I'd seen square dancing on television, and I'd nearly made up my mind to enjoy learning. But everybody was dancing in ordinary ways to ordinary music.

Nobody noticed us when we first arrived, but that wasn't surprising. The place was crowded, and getting worse every minute.

"Where do all these people come from?" I asked Heather.

"Abbey Falls, Fox Crossing, Perryville," she said. "There are kids here from all the towns in the county, I bet. They do this every summer, and everybody thinks it's great fun."

Micky Logan came in then, with a girl Heather introduced as Sandy Graham. A boy named Ken Dickerson brought them. A moment later, Paige Worth arrived, with a boy she called Colin. Two boys Colin knew asked us to sit at a table with them, and before I knew it, I'd been asked to dance. And not by somebody whose knuckles dragged on the floor, either. In spite of myself, I began enjoying the evening.

The first time all of us were sitting at the table together, Heather told everybody about Amelia's clown troupe in Seattle and how she wanted Amelia to teach some kids an act they could perform at the Centennial program.

Paige volunteered immediately. "I'd love it," she said. "I've always wanted to do something like that. And Colin wants to help, too."

"Colin certainly does not," Colin said, laughing. "I'd be awful. Get Thad to do it. He'd like wearing a wig and baggy pants."

"Sure I would," Thad scoffed.

"I want to help out," Sandy said.

"That makes three girls and one guy," Amelia said.

"Don't count on me!" Thad declared.

Heather poked him in the ribs. "Don't you dare let my cousin down," she said.

"Okay, then count me in," Thad said. "Heather has sharp fingers. Ow!"

"Three girls and one guy won't do it," Amelia said. "We absolutely need at least one more boy. Absolutely and no fooling around."

Everybody looked at Colin, and finally he nodded. "But I'll ruin everything," he said.

"It would be ideal if we could get another boy," Amelia said thoughtfully, looking around the table.

Rod Jackson, a grinning, brown-haired boy with hazel eyes, said, "I'll try it, but I get to quit if I start making an idiot out of myself. I promised myself I'd reform this summer."

"The whole point of being a clown," Amelia said,

"is that you can make an idiot out of yourself and nobody recognizes you, so nobody can blame you."

"Sounds perfect, since you put it that way," Rod said. He asked me to dance then, and when we were out in the middle of the floor, he said, "How come you don't want to be a clown?"

"I'm helping out in other ways," I said quickly. "Anyway, I don't have the right kind of humor to be a clown. That takes a special wacky humor. Like yours, I bet."

He laughed and put his hands on my shoulders. "I'm not sure I'm exactly wacky," he said. "Colin's the one who'll be good at that. But I'm willing to try, and I need something to keep me busy. My girl's in California for the summer."

He told me about his girl, and I told him about Brady. That took a good half hour, and then I was on my own again, back at the table.

Then the band stopped playing, and a tall man took the microphone. "Okay, folks," he said, "now we get down to the real reason we're all here. Ladies on the left, gents on the right. Here comes the Virginia reel."

They were going to square-dance after all. I saw Amelia, looking bewildered, being pulled to the left by Sandy. Heather was clear down at the end of the line, and I didn't see Micky anywhere. A girl with red hair gestured to me to get in line, but I shook my head. I didn't know anything about Virginia reels, and I didn't think a public place was where I wanted to learn.

The redhead came over to the table and grabbed my hand. "Come on, it's easy," she said. "Just do what everybody else does."

"No, I don't . . ." I began. But she wouldn't listen to me, and she was stronger than I. Before I knew it,

18

I was in line, between her and a short, blond girl who couldn't stop giggling.

"It's so much fun," she said. "You'll love it."

I looked across the room and saw the boys lining up. They actually seemed to be looking forward to it!

The music began, and the man at the microphone started calling out dance steps. I felt like a dolt, but I followed along, doing what the redhead did. We moved out across the room toward the boys, who were moving toward us, and we curtsied while the boys bowed! It was silly, but I liked it.

I had trouble not watching my feet, though. First of all, I was afraid I was going to make a horrible mistake. And I figured that if I didn't look directly at the boy coming toward me, I'd find it easier to pretend that he wasn't there, just in case.

"Hi."

I looked up. And straight into remarkable golden eyes. It was the boy who'd been at Thad's.

I couldn't say hi back. I couldn't say anything. The girls moved back then to the place where we'd started. Now the dance became more complicated. The redhead whispered in my ear, telling me what to do, because the man at the microphone was hard to understand since his instructions were in a strange sort of rhyme.

The reel took a long time. Sometimes I lost sight of the boy with golden eyes. But whenever I found him, he was looking at me, too. He was wearing a loose white shirt and jeans—and he was wonderful.

At last we joined hands. It was our turn to dance down between the lines together and back again.

When he let go of me so I could go back to my place, I felt almost dizzy. And disappointed. I'd wanted to go on holding his hands.

I looked across at him, and he smiled his slow, shy smile.

"Cute, isn't he?" the redhead said.

I swallowed and said, "Yes."

"His name is Toby Callahan," she said.

Toby. Suddenly, stupidly, I couldn't quit smiling.

When the reel was over, I headed back toward our table. I didn't dare look to see where Toby was going. I wanted him to be following me, but that was too much to hope for. He'd probably brought a girl to the dance. His steady girl. And she'd be beautiful and glamorous and smart and rich. She'd even be old enough to drive and have her own car. And she wouldn't be an orphan like me. She'd have parents and brothers and sisters. And everybody would be crazy about her.

"Hi again," he said.

I looked up at him, and I blushed. I, Erin, the biggest brat in the Whitney family, was actually blushing.

"Your name is Erin Whitney, you're fifteen, and you're an artist," he said. "You live with your aunt and uncle and a lot of cousins in Seattle, and once you socked a guy because he gave you a hard time. And you're going home at the end of August."

I shook my head, amazed. "How do you know all this?"

"I asked Thad to tell me everything he knew about you the other day. Heather talks about you a lot, he says. You're like her sister."

We'd stopped walking and were simply standing there, looking at each other.

"I don't know anything about you," I said.

"I can fix that," he said. "Can I take you home? I know where you live."

"I came with my cousins," I said. "I have to go home with them."

He kept *looking* at me. "Then maybe I can see you again. Do you like picnics? I know a great place, at Lost Lake. Would you like to go sometime?"

"I don't know," I said. What would Aunt Marsha and Uncle Will say about this? I knew they were every bit as strict as Aunt Ellen and Uncle Jock. Did Heather's family know this boy? Would they let me go?

"I'm sorry," he blurted. "I don't know what's wrong with me. I don't ask girls out very much, so I guess I've turned you off. Should I start over?"

I shook my head slowly, and once again that awful, unstoppable smile was back. Turn me off? Was he crazy?

"I'd have to ask my aunt and uncle—about the picnic, I mean," I said. "Maybe you could call me about it?"

"At Dr. Will Carver's house," he said. "I'll get the number out of the phone book."

"Yes," I said. My mouth had gone dry again. Dancers were whirling around us. The man at the microphone was calling out instructions.

Toby reached for my hand. "Do you want to dance again?"

"Not really," I said. "Maybe we could sit down somewhere."

He led me to a table against the wall. "Is this all right?"

His hand was trembling a little. I saw suddenly how awfully shy he was, how hard this had been for him.

"It's perfect," I said. "Now. You know everything about me. Tell me everything about you."

I didn't realize until an hour later, after the dance was over and my cousins and I were home again, that

Toby had talked for several minutes while we sat at the table—and he didn't tell me one thing about his family or where he lived. But I learned what books he liked, and what music. And I knew that he loved fried chicken but hated fish, and his favorite salad was potato with black olives in it.

"What happened to you at the dance?" Heather asked me when we got home. "You seemed to disappear." She was sitting on the edge of Amelia's bed, brushing her hair.

I pulled the elastic off the end of my braid and shook my hair loose over my shoulders. "I found somebody to talk to," I said.

"You should have danced more," Heather said. "I bet lots of the boys wanted to meet you."

"I don't think so," I said vaguely.

"I saw you dancing a reel with somebody," Amelia said. "Who was he?"

I shrugged.

"You can't meet anybody during a reel," Heather said. "There's too much going on."

I could have told them about Toby. But the storm Uncle Will predicted began suddenly, with a great flash of lightning and a roar of thunder.

A chill shook me. I crawled into bed without mentioning Toby, and I lay awake for a long time. I should have been happy, but I wasn't. I felt as if I were already saying good-bye.

Chapter 3

Dear Nick: Thanks for sending the weird old hat. I wish I could have gone to First Pick with you to shop for "new" school clothes. Maybe you can go again with me when I get back to Seattle. I can hardly wait to see the waiter's outfit you found. I told you the best stuff was always in the bin in the back corner!

Still alive in Fox Crossing,
The Girl in the Green Hat

On the following Wednesday, Bear and I were alone in the house most of the day. Uncle Will had an all-day committee meeting about the Centennial. Aunt Marsha went to Perryville with two of her friends to pick strawberries. Amelia was rehearsing with her new clown troupe. And Heather was late getting home from appointments with her dentist and her hairdresser.

The mailman had brought me a package from Nick, containing a fine green velvet hat with a wide, floppy brim—and a six-page letter complaining about Seattle weather, his braces, and the cost of a movie ticket. I'd finished the letter and was trying on the hat when Heather came home.

"Where did you get that wonderful, awful hat?" Heather asked as she came into the living room.

"My friend, Nicholas Brown, sent it to me," I

23

said. I was adjusting the hat brim and admiring myself thoroughly. "Which looks best—brim up or brim down?"

"Brim up," Heather said. "That way your face shows. The green is the exact color of your eyes."

"Our eyes," I corrected. I pushed the hat a little forward. "Nick found the hat in that used-clothing store I told you about when you were visiting in Seattle last spring."

"Where Amelia got clothes for the clowns?"

"Yes. I hope you've got something in Fox Crossing like First Pick. She's going to need stuff for the clowns she's training."

Heather flopped down on the sofa and leaned back. "Is that where she is? Did they decide to rehearse at Sandy's house after all?"

"Yes, because of the big family room in the basement. Want to go over and watch?"

Heather groaned. "Nope. On my way back from the hairdresser's I stopped by Micky's house to say good-bye, and now I'm so depressed, I can't decide whether to cry or scream."

"You should have gone with her," I said. I sat across from her and pushed my new hat to the back of my head. I loved the way it felt under my fingers, all soft and furry.

Heather shook her head. "No. Will told me to go, but I'd be letting him down. He's really counting on me to help out. I feel guilty for wishing sometimes that I could get out of it."

"I could have taken over for you for a few days," I said.

"You can't type," Heather said. "I'm bad enough, but you'd go crazy trying to hunt-and-peck all that stuff. Now I'm working on the dormitory lists. As soon as I finish, I've got to run down to the drugstore and make copies so everybody on the committee has one."

"Do it tomorrow," I said. "Anybody who's been to the dentist ought to get the rest of the day off."

"I didn't need any fillings," Heather said. "It wasn't the dentist who wore me out—it was the hairdresser. She's always trying to talk me into a new hairstyle, but what difference would a new style make? I hate the color of my hair. Why didn't I get nice reddish brown hair like you? Or pale blond hair. There was a girl there whose hair was so gorgeous that I felt like pulling my purse over mine to hide it."

"Your hair is beautiful," I said generously, and meaning it. "You and Paige are lucky to have that shiny, light brown hair."

"Ugh," Heather said. "I wish it were blond. Blond and long, like the girl in the shop had. I couldn't tell if the color was natural or not, but who cares?"

I studied my cousin carefully. "You could lighten it. People do it all the time."

"I asked my hairdresser how much it costs," Heather admitted. "I'd have to save my allowance for a thousand years, because I can promise you that Mom and Will would never pay for anything like that. And then I'd have to have touch-ups every five minutes, practically."

"Do it all yourself," I said.

"I could . . ." Heather began, but Amelia came home then, interrupting our conversation with big groans and complaints about how impossible it was to teach a basketball player to turn cartwheels when he didn't want to learn, or to stop Sandy from laughing all the time.

"I'm so tired I could die," she finished up.

"Then you don't want to help me fix dinner," I said.

25

She gawked at me. "Are you crazy? I can barely walk."

I laughed. "That was a joke. Aunt Marsha said she'd bring home take-out food."

"I'm too tired to eat," Amelia said. "All I want to do is sleep, for at least a week."

"Can't," I said. "You and I are going to help Heather change the color of her hair."

Amelia sat up straight. "You mean it? Really? What color?"

"Pale blond," Heather said, sounding more confident now. "If you guys will help, I can do it here and save a lot of money."

Amelia looked at me. "You know how to do this?"

"Nope," I said, "but there must be instructions on the boxes of bleach. We'll walk over to the drugstore and read all the labels."

"I'll change my hair, too," Amelia said. "I'm bored to death with how I look."

"I'll call Paige and see if she wants to try it," Heather said. "We like doing things that make us look alike."

Both of them looked at me. "Hey," I said weakly. "My hair is awfully long for experiments."

"Right," Amelia said. "Darn it. Looks like you get left out."

"I think I can live with it," I said, laughing.

"Wow," Amelia blurted. "The hat. I must be going blind. You've got a new one. Where did you find it?"

"Nick sent it to me," I said.

"It would look great on blond hair," Amelia said.

"I'm a coward," I said. We all laughed. But I gave some serious thought about cutting my hair and turning it a different color. A glamorous color.

No, not glamorous. That wouldn't suit. But if I had

pale blond hair . . . no. I'd look stupid, and when I got back to Seattle, Nick would die laughing. Little twerp.

Aunt Marsha and Uncle Will got home within five minutes of each other, and we ate our take-out chicken in the backyard, in the shade of a big willow.

"Any plans for this evening?" Aunt Marsha asked us.

I'd expected Heather to tell her mother what she and Amelia were planning, but instead, she shook her head and said, "Nothing, really. We'll probably take Bear for a walk."

"I'm so sick of talking to people—present company excepted," Uncle Will said, "that I'm going to bed early with a book."

"The meeting was that bad?" Aunt Marsha asked him.

"Problems with the mayor," Uncle Will said. "Nothing we didn't handle, though. At least, so far."

Amelia and I weren't paying too much attention to this, but Heather was. "I can't stand that man," she said. "He's done nothing to help and everything to make trouble."

Uncle Will shrugged. "If I'd known how important it was to him to head up the Centennial committee, I'd have turned it down and recommended him. But I didn't know until after I'd been involved for weeks."

"It's not your fault," Heather said crossly. "He butts in to everything. Paige says that her father might run against him in the next election. If he does, I'm going to help out."

"You'll be an asset to him," Uncle Will said. "So Ed Worth is planning to run against Callahan. Interesting."

Callahan. But that was Toby's last name!

Callahan was a common name. This was just a

coincidence. Toby couldn't possibly be related to the man my family disliked so much. He was so nice. And the mayor was so awful.

"Does he have a family, this Callahan?" I asked cautiously.

"He has a wife, but I hardly know her," Aunt Marsha said. "She manages that dress shop across from the videotape store."

"And he has a son," Heather said.

My heart almost stopped.

"I forget his name," Heather went on. "He doesn't go to school here—he goes to boarding school somewhere. But I saw him at the dance Saturday night. Thad knows him."

"What's he like?" Amelia asked.

Heather shrugged. "Don't ask me, ask Erin. She danced with him. I saw her."

Everybody stared at me. I shrugged, too. "I danced with several boys I don't know. What does he look like?"

"He's dark, and tall. He doesn't look much like his dad."

"That's no help," I said. "Practically every boy is tall and dark."

"Except Thad," Heather said. "And at least twenty other boys I could name. Honestly, Erin. Why don't you pay more attention when you're at a dance?"

"She's impossible," Amelia said. "At home, she dates Brady Harris once in a while, but they're like brother and sister."

"How do you know?" I demanded hotly.

"Are you three sure you want us listening to this conversation?" Uncle Will asked solemnly.

"Brother and sister," I muttered. I got up and started clearing the table. "Brother and sister. Fat lot you know."

I carried plates into the kitchen, Bear following behind and slobbering. I couldn't think straight. Toby was the mayor's son. And the mayor was trying hard to make himself my uncle's enemy.

And Toby said he would call me sometime and take me on a picnic. Obviously I could forget that idea.

My cousins and I did go for a walk after dinner, but we didn't take Bear. We stopped for Paige and then headed straight for the drugstore, and we spent the next half hour reading labels on the boxes of hair lightener.

"This all sounds pretty complicated," Heather said. "And it will cost a lot if each of us gets a box."

"I don't like all the warnings about not getting the stuff into your eyes," Amelia said. "It says here you're supposed to call a doctor."

"There has to be an easier way to get blond," Paige said.

"Bleach, like the stuff we use in the laundry?" I asked.

They looked interested for a moment, but then shook their heads. "It smells awful," Heather said.

"I'd be scared to try it," Amelia said. "Remember what happened to the brown socks Mom accidentally mixed in with the towels? They turned out orange."

"People used to use peroxide," I said. "I remember reading about it. They mixed peroxide with soap flakes."

"Soap flakes?" Paige asked. "Don't you mean laundry detergent?"

I shrugged. "I don't think so."

"Soap and detergent are the same thing," Heather said.

"I doubt it," I told her. "But why don't we ask the clerk?"

We did. She was lots older than Aunt Marsha, and she said she hadn't seen soap flakes for a long time.

"Would detergent powder do the same job?" Amelia asked her.

"Maybe," the woman said. "What do you want to wash?"

"Nothing. We were just curious," Heather said.

The four of us went back to the hair-care counter and had a consultation. Soap flakes didn't seem to be easily available.

"We'll just go ahead and use laundry detergent," Heather said. "What could go wrong? And Mom has a big bottle of peroxide in the downstairs medicine cabinet. We use it for cuts and scrapes and bug bites. We won't even have to buy anything."

We left the drugstore pleased with ourselves, especially since we didn't have to spend money. "Since it's free," I said, "maybe I'll try it, too. You know, bleach some streaks in my hair. That might look nice."

Excited, we ran the rest of the way home. Paige called her mother for permission to spend the night, and we were all set.

And then we sat around and waited—and waited—for Aunt Marsha to go to bed.

She stayed up until nearly ten. The minute we heard the shower running in the upstairs bath, we ran to the downstairs bath and grabbed the peroxide out of the medicine cabinet.

"Now what?" Amelia asked, looking at me.

"Gee, I wish you weren't expecting me to know all the answers," I complained. "What if I give you the wrong advice?"

"Then you'll look funny, too," Heather said.

We took the box of detergent powder from the laundry room, got a big bowl from the kitchen, and carried them to the bathroom. I mixed detergent and peroxide together into a gooey mess.

"This doesn't look too promising, pals," I said.

Paige stuck one finger in the mess. "At least it won't run into our eyes. That was the idea, wasn't it?"

"I guess," I said vaguely. "How long do you suppose it takes?"

"Don't you know?" demanded Heather.

"Of course not!" I exclaimed. "I never tried it."

"Well, let's try it now," Amelia said.

She went first, scooping out a handful of the goo and spreading it over her hair, working it in with her fingers.

Heather went next. Her hair was a little longer, and she needed more goo. Paige used most of what was left, and then apologized to me for taking so much.

I didn't mind, because I only wanted blond streaks. I took down my braid and selected a couple of strands of hair for treatment. When I finished, I looked like a witch with horns.

"Now we wait," Heather said.

We watched TV in the kitchen for an hour. Every once in a while Amelia or Heather would soak a paper towel in water and scrape some of the mess off a strand of her hair. The color stayed the same—but the detergent foamed a lot if the towels were too wet.

"Are you sure about all this?" Paige asked me.

"No," I said, as I tried to clean off my own hair. "My hair is exactly the same color that I started out with, but I don't think I'll ever get the detergent out of it."

"It's been more than an hour now," Heather said. "Don't you think that it should have worked by now?"

"Yes," I said. "We'd better wash this stuff out of our hair before we suddenly go bald or something."

"Maybe you really do need to use soap, not detergent," Amelia said.

"Maybe it wasn't peroxide that you're supposed to use," Heather said, scowling at me.

"I'm sure it's peroxide," I said. "I don't know what's wrong."

We decided to shower the stuff out of our hair, and Heather went first. From behind the shower curtain, we heard her groan, then swear, then burst into tears.

"What's wrong?" I cried.

"I'm up to my knees in foam, and my hair is still full of this stuff!"

Amelia, Paige, and I exchanged a look. The goo was drying on their hair—I could see it. This was horrible!

By the time Heather's hair was clean, there was no hot water left downstairs. But Heather said that the bathrooms upstairs had a separate hot water heater, so we rushed up there, and Amelia got into the shower first.

It took nearly half an hour for the stuff to wash out of her hair. By that time, Paige and I had no choice but to shower in ice-cold water.

All my long hair was cold and wet. I was afraid my skin would stay blue permanently. And by that time it was nearly midnight.

"What on earth are you girls doing?" Aunt Marsha asked when we came out of the bathroom.

"Fooling around with our hair," Heather said.

"Well, do it in the morning," Aunt Martha said. She stared hard at me. "It will take you forever to blow-dry that hair, Erin. You'll be exhausted tomorrow."

I couldn't think of a thing to say, so I padded past her, shivering inside the towel I had wrapped around me.

Dumb, dumb, dumb, I thought.

But it *was* peroxide that you were supposed to use! I was certain of it. What had gone wrong?

The next morning, after Heather went off to the den to start work, Amelia, Paige, and I had a long, important, whispered conversation upstairs.

"We need expert advice," I said.

"Yeah, from somebody who really knows about peroxide and stuff like that," Amelia said.

"Not the woman in the drugstore," Paige said. "She'll wonder why we don't buy the stuff in the boxes."

"Maybe we should," Amelia said. "This peroxide idea doesn't work."

"Maybe Aunt Marsha would know why it didn't," I said. "After all, she's a nurse. She must know all about peroxide."

"You ask her," Paige said.

"No, let Amelia," I said.

"Are you crazy?" Amelia demanded. "She'll want to know why I'm asking all the questions. And I really don't think we ought to tell anybody ahead of time that we're going to bleach our hair."

"Then what are we supposed to do?" Paige asked.

"Nobody has to do anything today," I said. "We can wait and see what we can find out."

"Oh, darn," Amelia grouched. "I need to do something different about how I look."

"Wear your clown nose all the time," I said, but she didn't think I was funny.

That was the end of the good times for that day. After breakfast, Amelia, Heather, and I walked Paige home, and then we strolled a few blocks north to the shopping district. Heather wanted to show us the new shoe store before she went back to work.

We were standing on the sidewalk admiring a pair of boots in the window when the mayor came up. He didn't look friendly.

"Hello, Mr. Callahan," Heather said.

"I heard at the print shop that you ordered posters for the Centennial," he said. He glanced briefly at Amelia, and a little longer at me, probably because of my hat. His glance turned to a scowl. I squared my hat on my head and scowled back.

"Yes, I ordered posters," Heather babbled in response to his comment. I hated the way he could make her so nervous.

Mr. Callahan's face flushed. "What makes Will think that he's going to use City Park for the Centennial Fair?"

"He got a permit from the city council," Heather said. She looked alarmed, and I wasn't sure why. I didn't know that much about the Centennial yet.

"So I hear," Mr. Callahan said. "But maybe the council made a mistake." I could see that he enjoyed making Heather so miserable. "Maybe," he went on, "they will have to reconsider."

And with that, he wheeled around and walked off.

"What was that all about?" Amelia asked.

Heather shook her head angrily. "Who knows?" He's always griping about something. Nobody cares that his great-grandfather was one of the college founders. Will's the one who loves this whole Centennial idea."

I watched Mr. Callahan turn the corner. He thought he was a whole army, all by himself. Jerk. What would happen if he knew that his son liked one of Will Carver's nieces?

"Are you going to tell your stepfather what he said?" Amelia asked Heather.

"No," Heather said. "Will's got enough to worry about."

I didn't agree, and her decision made me nervous. People handle disasters better if they're prepared ahead of time. And Mayor Callahan looked like somebody who was capable of throwing disasters around like mud balls.

Chapter 4

Dear Nick: Amelia is having trouble with her new clowns. One won't quit laughing, and another keeps saying somebody else's lines. The rest are about as funny as a headache. She's ready to run away, and so am I—but for a different reason. I'll tell you later. Maybe.

> Wish you were here (Really!)
> Erin

One cool evening after dinner, Heather, Amelia, and I walked around town nailing up college Centennial posters. It wasn't as if nobody in town knew about the celebration. But, Heather said, the committee decided that the posters would keep everybody excited about it. As a bonus, any strangers driving through town would find out about the event.

At nearly every place we put up a poster, somebody stopped to talk to us. I saw lots of the kids who'd been at the dance, but not Toby. And I didn't dare ask about him, either. I certainly couldn't have my cousins wondering if something was going on. And I wasn't sure I wanted anything to happen between Toby and me.

But what I wanted didn't matter anyway. He didn't call me. I don't know why I believed he would. When I remembered the night of the dance—which was practically all the time—it seemed to me that he'd been sincere. But maybe that was just the way he acted. Or maybe he'd realized how upset his father would be when he found out that we knew each other.

Or maybe I had only imagined how he'd looked at me, talked to me. Held my hand.

Lots of the stores were still open the evening we went out with the posters, so my cousins and I asked in all of them if we could put some in the windows. Nearly everybody said we could.

Some of the kids we'd run into walked along with us, so by the time we'd put up all the posters, we'd collected a nice, friendly crowd. Heather called Thad and Paige from the public phone outside the pizza place, and they joined us. Without intending to, we ended up with a party on our hands.

Half a ton of pepperoni later, we were all sitting around our tables and talking when Toby Callahan arrived.

He slid into the empty chair next to Thad and said, "Sorry it took me so long."

"That's okay," Thad said. "There's still pizza left. Go get yourself something to drink and come back and meet Erin and Amelia, from Seattle."

Toby nodded to me. "I know Erin already."

I watched him walk up to the counter to order. Amelia jabbed me in my ribs. "Who's that?" she asked.

"Toby Callahan," I said, hoping Heather wouldn't hear.

But she did. "So you do know Toby," she said.

"Well, just from the dance," I said. My face burned, and I hoped my blush didn't show.

He came back and sat down. He was far enough away, on my side of the table, so that I couldn't see him without leaning forward. I sat there listening to him being introduced to Amelia and exchanging a few polite words.

Why hadn't he ever called me?

Why did I care so much?

No matter how hard I tried, I couldn't make much sense of anything anybody said. And when the manager came around and told us that it was late and he had to close, I was glad.

It was dark outside now, cool and dark. I waited by the door for Heather to say good-bye to everybody—except Thad, because he was coming home with us—and for Amelia to finish her lecture to some of her laughing, disrespectful students about how serious the clown act rehearsals were supposed to be.

"Walk you home?"

Toby had come up behind me. I whirled around and looked up at him, unable to answer.

"I like your hat," he said. "It matches your eyes."

I stood there forever and finally said, "Thanks."

"So can I walk you home?" he asked again.

What was I supposed to do? His father was Heather's enemy. The family's enemy.

Amelia was staring at me. Thad stood with his arm across Heather's shoulders, and they were watching, too.

"Erin and Toby, come on with us," Thad said, putting an end to my misery.

Thad walked between Amelia and Heather, ahead of us. He kept up a steady conversation, barely audible to me, and gradually the three of them drew away from us.

We drifted along the sidewalk, dawdling between the pools of light cast by the streetlights, not talking. It took two blocks before I could breathe properly.

"I'm sorry I haven't called," he said finally. "But

I've been working at my dad's farm on the other side of Lost Lake. There's no phone there.''

''I didn't expect you to call,'' I said. Then I realized how abrupt I must have sounded, so I added, ''After all, we hardly know each other.''

''And you'll be going home at the end of summer,'' he said.

''And you'll be going back to boarding school,'' I said.

He glanced down at me, then away. ''Yes.'' He didn't say anything more for a long while, and then he said, ''We don't have much time, do we?''

''No,'' I said.

Oh, this is crazy, I told myself. Crazy. Dangerous. *Delicious.*

I saw my cousins and Thad walking far ahead under a streetlight, turning the corner toward Heather's house. ''We're almost there,'' I said.

''I'd better not come in,'' he said. ''Would you like to see Lost Lake tomorrow? My dad's going to be out of town . . .'' He paused and glanced away, as if he was embarrassed. ''I could drive over and pick you up at ten. I'll bring lunch for us. Or if you like, we could ride bikes. Maybe Heather would let you use hers. Or I could borrow one for you.''

''Let's go on bikes.''

We were at the corner. He took my hand for a moment, then let it go quickly. I heard footsteps on the pavement, turned my head, and saw Thad walking back toward us.

''Good night,'' Toby said. ''See you tomorrow.''

I ran off, only waving at Thad as I passed him.

What was I doing, promising to go to Lost Lake with Toby tomorrow? Did I dare tell Heather and Amelia?

I had to tell them. It wasn't something I looked forward to doing, believe me.

They took it better than I'd hoped. The three of us were sitting in the kitchen when I explained.

"His father will have a fit when he finds out," Heather said.

"What about Uncle Will?" I asked. I was more worried about my uncle.

"My stepdad's a great guy," Heather said. "He won't care. He'd like to be friends with Mr. Callahan, if it was possible. It's Mr. Callahan who causes the problems, not Will."

"What about you guys?" I asked. "How do you feel?"

Heather shrugged. "Toby is nice. Sorta shy. I don't know him at all, but Thad wouldn't be friends with him if he was a jerk. Colin likes him, too."

Amelia was looking down at the table, drawing invisible circles on the wood. "What about Brady?"

I nearly burst into tears. "You know that I like Brady a lot," I said. "He's been wonderful to me. If it hadn't been for him, I don't know what would have happened to me last spring. But . . ."

"But what?" Amelia asked. "I'm not mad at you, I just want to understand what you're thinking—what's happening to you. Honestly, Erin, I could practically feel electricity in the air when you and Toby looked at each other."

I shook my head. "I can't explain what's going on between us. I hardly know him, and I can't stand his father. And I'm going home to Seattle in a few weeks."

"Back to Brady," Heather said.

"No, not back to Brady!" I cried. "It's not as if we were going steady. He's never even talked about anything like that."

"But you like him," Amelia said.

I nodded.

"And you like Toby," Heather said.

I didn't answer at first. Then, finally, I said, "I could, I guess. This is all so stupid."

"I think it's called love at first sight," Amelia said.

I stared hard at her. "Amelia, I don't believe in stuff like that."

Amelia shrugged. "Okay, so don't believe in it. But that's what it's called."

Telling Uncle Will about Toby and the picnic would be harder. I chose the next morning after breakfast, while Uncle Will was drinking his second cup of coffee and watching Bear chase her shadow around the backyard.

"Toby is a nice boy," Uncle Will said when I finished. "He knows the woods around the lake better than anyone else. You won't get lost with him."

All he cared about was whether or not I got lost? Uncle Will was every bit as imperturbable as Heather had said.

When I told Aunt Marsha, she only grinned and said, "Don't let the mayor catch you flirting with his only son. That's Romeo and Juliet stuff."

Heather went off a few minutes later to check her dormitory lists against somebody else's lists. Paige, loaded down with bags of old clothes that she'd found in her uncle's garage, came to consult with Amelia on important clown stuff. Both of them left a few minutes later, dragging the bags behind them.

Aunt Marsha drove off to the free clinic, and Uncle Will began making endless phone calls from the extension in his den.

I waited. I changed clothes, discarding jeans for white shorts, then changing back into jeans, then switching to red shorts. I picked through my used-hat collection and finally settled on a small straw hat with a rather ragged red rose pinned under the brim.

At exactly ten o'clock, Toby rang the doorbell. Uncle Will let him in. I was numb with shock, frozen on the stair landing, staring at my reflection in the oval mirror on the wall.

I, Erin Whitney, did not believe in love at first sight. But suddenly I couldn't stop smiling. That Toby Callahan would want to take me biking to Lost Lake seemed like the most amazing thing that had ever happened to anyone since the beginning of time, and maybe for a couple of eternities before that.

"I like that hat, too," he said when he saw me. He was looking straight into my eyes.

"Erin has many hats," Uncle Will said. "She surprises us nearly every day."

He walked out on the porch with us. Toby had strapped a picnic basket to his bike, and Uncle Will asked him what he'd brought along to eat. While they talked about food, I wheeled Heather's bike out of the garage.

As Toby and I rode away, I looked back and saw Uncle Will watching us. His expression was so odd that I nearly turned around and asked him what was wrong.

But I didn't want to know.

I was afraid to know. Romeo and Juliet stuff. Maybe I wasn't strong enough for trouble like that.

Chapter 5

Dear Nick: I miss you, too. There's nobody here
I can talk to. I mean *really* talk to. And I have
an awful hunch that by the time I get home, I'll
have secrets to keep.

Strange things are happening here,
Erin

Toby and I rode north, first on a two-lane highway
and then along a narrow, winding road that rose
slightly. There were pastures on both sides of this
road, and several times we crossed small bridges over
shallow creeks rimmed with willow trees.

Mostly we rode in silence, side by side unless a
car was coming, which wasn't often. I caught Toby
looking at me several times, but then, he caught
me looking at him, too.

I didn't feel much like smiling anymore. It wasn't
that I'd stopped being happy. It was as if I were beginning a strange journey, and I had no idea how it
would turn out or when it would end.

"Are you getting tired?" Toby asked after we'd
been riding more than half an hour.

"No."

"The road levels out pretty soon."

"Fine. How much farther will we go before we see
your dad's farm?"

"We aren't taking that road," Toby said. "The

43

farm's on the other side of Lost Lake. We're going to the picnic grounds on the island. But we'll be able to see the farm from the far side, across the water.''

"How do we get to the island?'' I asked.

"There's a footbridge,'' he said. "Just wide enough for us to cross single file.''

A truck pulling an empty horse trailer passed us. The driver called out something to Toby and waved. Toby laughed and waved back. Three little kids on foot came from the other direction, followed by three dogs. Toby stopped to talk to them, and I could see how pleased they were. The dogs greeted him, too, like old friends.

Out here, everybody seemed to know Toby and like him. In town, he stayed quietly in the shadows. I couldn't help but wonder if this had more to do with his father than his going away to boarding school every fall.

In another fifteen minutes, we reached a clearing beside a wide, crescent-shaped lake. Three cars were parked there. On the far side of the clearing, a woman was leading a small boy across a footbridge. The child stopped every couple of feet, to hang on the wobbly railing and lean out over the water. Finally his mother picked him up and carried him.

We parked our bikes near the cars. Toby unbuckled the nylon straps that held his picnic basket in place. "I hope you like the food I brought,'' he said.

"I'm hungry already,'' I admitted.

"Then we'll eat as soon as we get there,'' he said, laughing.

The lake was still and dark. The mossy footbridge was made of wood, and the railing shook under my hand.

"The bridge will be taken down at the end of summer," Toby said, after I looked up at him, unable to hide my worry.

"Are you sure it's safe?" I asked.

"For now," he said. "It can't take any more stormy seasons, though. I wish the county would replace it."

"You mean there won't be a way to get to the island after this summer?" I asked.

Toby shook his head. "Nope. They're turning the island into a bird sanctuary. I don't mind. I guess I come here more than anybody else, and I'll miss it, but I'll be able to see it from here or around on the other side, by Dad's farm. And I'll know that the birds will have a good place where they won't be disturbed."

I took my first step out on the bridge, expecting it to cave in under me. But it didn't, and so I walked across, head up, and I didn't worry any longer. Toby was close behind.

On the other side, I saw a clearing in the woods where long ago someone had built rough tables and benches. There was even an outdoor fireplace, but it looked as if it hadn't been used for years.

The woman and her little boy were out of sight, but other people had spread picnic lunches out on two of the tables. Usually, in picnic areas, half the people have radios or tape players blasting, but no one here did. I guess they'd learned to appreciate the sounds of the woods.

They all knew Toby, and he introduced me around. Then we took a table near the fireplace, and Toby opened the basket. "I've got three kinds of sandwiches, and cheese, and apples, and crackers, and soft drinks, and—"

"Stop," I begged. "I'll die of starvation before you finish your list."

He laughed and handed me a paper plate. "Okay," he said. "Eat first and talk later."

While we ate, the mother and her little boy came back. They knew Toby, too, and they took the table closest to us. The mother pulled their lunch from her backpack.

"I have jelly sandwiches," the boy told us. "And an orange and two cookies."

"Sounds good," Toby said.

The little boy stared at me. "That's a funny hat, girl," he said.

"Brady!" his mother said, frowning. "Don't be rude."

Brady.

I wrapped up the last of my lunch in a paper napkin and put it in the basket. I didn't want to remember Brady Harris, far away in Seattle, at a time like this. I didn't want to think about anybody except Toby and me.

We left the basket on the table and walked along a trail that led across the center of the island, between tall firs and ancient maples. I wished that I'd remembered to bring my sketchbook. The simple truth was that I was lucky I'd remembered to bring my head.

It didn't take long before we were on the other shore, looking across at Mayor Callahan's farm.

"There's a lot more water to cross here," I said.

"Yes. A footbridge wouldn't work out too well. But sometimes I come over in my canoe. I keep it stored in an old shed behind the barn."

"Will you come across when this is officially a bird sanctuary?"

"No, afraid not," he told me. "No one can come then."

We sat down at the edge of the water and looked over at the farm. Several black and white cows grazed in the pasture. I saw a large barn and several smaller buildings in the distance.

"Where's the house?" I asked.

"There's a bunkhouse on the other side of the orchard," Toby said. "The hired man lives there. And that's where I stay when I'm working here."

"Do you like it?"

"Yes. My dad doesn't, though. He only keeps the farm because it belonged to his family."

I felt the warm wind spring up at almost the same instant I heard faint and distant wind chimes, and I laughed. "Listen!" I said. "Someone's put up glass chimes on the other side of the lake."

"I did, in one of the trees at the far end of the pasture. If the wind picks up, you'll hear something else that will surprise you."

"What?" I asked.

"Wait and see," he said. "If I tell you about it now, I'll spoil it."

But the wind died down instead, and I forgot about Toby's surprise for a while.

We talked about our schools. I'd learned to like mine, finally, after some hard times. Toby, however, seemed merely resigned to his.

"Boarding school is okay," he said. "I'd rather be home, but my dad went to this school in Massachusetts, and he and my mother want me to do the same thing."

"Did you ever go to public school?" I asked.

"Sure. Until eighth grade. I'm a senior this year, and then I'll go to college. I guess I'll have to wait a long time before I can live here."

"You want to be a farmer?" I asked, surprised.

Now he smiled and looked truly happy for the first time. "Yes. But I promised my parents that I'd finish

47

college and then make up my mind for certain. Except that . . ."

"It's already made up," I finished for him.

Suddenly I heard the wind chimes again, singing like a glass harp in the trees across the water. And then behind me, in the island trees, I heard hundreds of birds trilling. As long as the wind chimes rippled, the birds sang.

"Starlings," Toby said, looking back over his shoulder. "They like the sound of the wind chimes. When it gets loud enough, they sing back to it. Sometimes, when I'm on the other side, I shake it just to get the birds started. Once I did that on a misty morning when I could hardly see the island. The birds' voices seemed to come out of another world. Out of another time."

The wind chimes fell silent, and so did the birds. Then, a moment later, the chorus began again.

"How long ago did you put up the chimes?" I asked.

"Just last spring," he said. "Mom found the pieces in an old trunk in the attic. I put them back together again. I thought the orchard would be a good place for it, that it might scare the birds away from the fruit. But they liked the sound, and ate the fruit anyway. We've got so much, though, that I don't mind."

"Does your dad feel the same way?" I asked.

Toby had been looking across the water at the farm, but now he glanced away, toward a stand of firs on the west. "No. Dad resents losing anything to the birds. He didn't want the island turned into a sanctuary, because that will attract even more birds, but there was no way he could stop it. It was the county council's decision. A lot of people from the college worked hard to convince them that the birds needed a safe nesting area."

"My uncle, too?" I asked.

Toby nodded.

So Mayor Callahan hated Will for more than one reason, I thought. "I guess your dad wouldn't like it if he knew you'd brought me out here today," I said. "Right?"

Toby shrugged. "Hey, we're here, and that's what counts. We shouldn't worry about what happens next."

Then he looked down at me and grinned and pushed his hair away from his forehead. The sight of him absolutely stunned me. I didn't know what to call the feeling. All I knew was that I didn't want it to stop.

We sat there for a long time, watching birds, and Toby could identify all of them, from a tiny brown one with a body half the length of my little finger to the long-legged heron who stared suspiciously at us from the shallows. Again, I was sorry that I'd forgotten my sketchbook.

Every once in a while the wind would pick up, and the chimes and the birds would sing back and forth to each other, from island to orchard.

The spell was cast. I came out to the island as cynical Erin Whitney, whose parents had been killed when she was ten, and who had hardly ever trusted anybody since then—and I left the island practically believing that I was enchanted.

An enchanted princess with her prince, trying to run away from what was coming.

Dear Nick: Remember how funny Amelia's clown
act was last spring? Well, the act she's trying to
put together here is a disaster. It's so awful that
she's going to get laughs for all the wrong reasons. Heather isn't happy, either. She says that
the Centennial came a hundred years too soon.
And I wish I'd gone to Oklahoma with my family. I'd tell you why if I thought there was half
a chance you'd understand and not laugh.

Struck by lightning,
Erin

Heather, Amelia, and I were sitting outside in the
dark one warm night in late July when suddenly I
realized that nobody had said a word for at least fifteen minutes. That had to be a record for silence for
the three of us.

"Hello?" I said. "Is there anyone out here on the
deck besides me? I'm beginning to feel like I'm the
last person alive in the whole universe."

"Sorry, Erin," Heather said. "I guess I was feeling sorry for myself, and I liked it too much to quit.
Gosh, I'm thirsty. Is there any juice left in the
pitcher?"

I took the pitcher off the table and shook it. I heard
something sloshing, but I didn't hear the clink of ice
cubes. "There's juice, but I bet it's watery and luke-
warm."

"Who cares?" Heather said. "Push it toward me. Anybody else want some?"

"Ugh," Amelia said. "I've been stuffing my stomach all evening, and after that huge dinner I ate, too. Pretty soon I won't need padding in my clown suit to look fat, because I'll be enormous. An enormous, boring clown. A humongously stupid clown with ugly plain brown hair. I might as well be dead."

"Well, save room in the casket for me, because I'm working myself to death," Heather grumbled. "Who would have believed that nothing ever gets done in this town unless somebody types a hundred lists and letters about it. Sometimes I wonder if anybody actually reads all that stuff."

"Your stepfather told you not to do so much," I said.

"I know, I know," Heather said. "It's not his fault. But things keep going wrong, and there's nobody else to run all the errands. At least, there's nobody else who's willing except Erin. And she doesn't know any of the people involved or where they are. Sorry, Erin. I appreciate what you try to do, but you can't be expected to find the sanitation department manager if he isn't in his office, and so you wasted a whole afternoon looking for him so you could give him that envelope. Anybody who lived in Fox Crossing would have known that he works part-time in the lumberyard."

"I still don't understand why you needed to give anything to him," I said. "What does a sanitation department manager have to do with a Centennial celebration?"

"Don't ask," Heather said. "It involves public rest rooms, and it's just too revolting to discuss on a gorgeous night like this. Anyway, Will said he'd take care of it. Why is it so hard to get people to cooperate?''

"Don't ask me," Amelia said. "I can't get any of my clowns to take things seriously. All they want to do is fool around. They won't believe me when I tell them that the act will take practice and then some more practice. Being funny doesn't just happen, like hiccups. You have to plan every single laugh. Erin, won't you please reconsider and be a clown? I am *begging* you, if you've noticed."

I leaned back in my chair and stared up at the stars. "No, no, a million times no, I won't be a part of your act. I would be a rotten clown. The audience would throw stuff at me. Maybe even knives and bombs. But I'll make costumes and props, and run errands, and fix snacks."

I hadn't been paying too much attention to the conversation, not even my part of it. The sky was the darkest blue I'd ever seen, almost black, and the stars seemed larger than they did in Seattle. In the west, an especially large star hung over the horizon, almost close enough to touch. I would have reached out my hand, but my cousins already thought I'd been more than a little bit weird in those last few days.

How many people on this side of the earth are looking up at the stars right now? I wondered. Has Toby seen them tonight? Is he a star watcher, like me?

If he and I were the only two looking up at this exact moment, would that be a sign that everything can turn out all right between us? Is it possible? Or am I crazy even to be thinking about it?

"Erin, are you asleep?" Amelia asked, half laughing.

"Certainly not!" I said. I sat up straight. "I was thinking about—things."

"Not about clowns and Centennials, I bet," she said. "You sighed the biggest sigh I ever heard."

"I was thinking that it must be nearly midnight, and we ought to be in bed." I got out of my chair and stretched. "Aren't you two tired?"

"I'm so tired, I'm positive I won't be able to fall asleep," Heather said. "I'll lie awake all night worrying about not getting enough rest."

"Well, you've got to try," Amelia said. "Erin's right. Let's go to bed. We aren't solving any of our problems by sitting out here in the dark."

They went inside ahead of me, and I lingered for just a moment, to stare out at the biggest star. Was it magical? Should I make a wish?

No. Somebody said that we should be careful what we wish for because we might get it.

And I didn't really know what I wanted.

The next morning Paige came by for Amelia after breakfast, and they went off together, talking about somebody's big yellow satin pants, and who was going to sew on sequins.

Heather watched them go, and it occurred to me that she might be sorry she wasn't a part of the clown troupe after all.

"You could be, you know," I said.

"Could be what?" she asked. "Hey, do you want the rest of this yogurt?" Yogurt was her favorite breakfast. The rest of us wouldn't touch it.

"I feel like Uncle Will does about yogurt," I said. "I don't want to eat something full of little living things."

"It wouldn't bother you if you would quit talking about stuff like that," she said. "Why don't you feel sorry for strawberries or bologna sandwiches?"

"Because they don't have mothers," I said. "Yogurt might have whole families. The least you could do is hit it with a hammer first and stun it.''

"I'll finish it myself, if you're going to act like that," she said. "Just shut up about it." But I noticed that she wasn't swallowing very easily.

Earlier, Uncle Will and Aunt Marsha had left together to shop for groceries. I'd promised to clean up the kitchen alone, because Heather had a dozen phone calls to make, so I began stacking plates.

"I could be *what?*" Heather demanded, suddenly remembering what I'd said before the Great Yogurt Debate began. "I can't stand it when somebody says half a sentence."

"You could be part of the clown troupe," I said. "Mostly they rehearse in the afternoons."

"Amelia is gone every morning, too," Heather said. "With Paige."

"Yes, but they're not rehearsing then. They're fixing costumes and writing lines for the others," I said. "Uncle Will can manage by himself in the afternoons when all the kids get together, I bet. If he has some big crashing emergency, I'll help."

But she shook her head. "No, it's too late for me to join the clowns." She got to her feet with a groan and headed down the hall toward the den. "If the president of the United States phones me, tell him he'll have to wait until fall if he wants help. If Thad phones, tell him I don't have time to walk Bear this morning, so he'll have to take Heidi out alone."

Bear, hearing her name, raised her head and looked around.

"No walk today," I told her. "You and I will have to make ourselves useful around here."

The phone rang, and I groaned louder than Heather had.

"Tell the president to call back in the fall," I muttered while I crossed the floor. "Tell Thad she can't walk with the dogs today." I lifted the receiver. "Hello?"

A man demanded to speak to Uncle Will. I explained that he would be back in an hour or so. And then I added, "Is this about the Centennial?"

"You bet it is," the man said. "Are you Will's daughter?"

"I'm his niece," I said. "Can I help you?" I could hear Heather typing, and I wanted to spare her as much as I could.

"This is Henry Barker," the man said. "Tell Will that the mayor has asked the town council to cancel our park permit. And ask him to call me right away."

"Oh," I said, trying to sound intelligent. "Okay, I'll give him the message as soon as he gets here."

The man hung up, and I began writing the message on the notepad on the counter.

"Who was that?" Heather asked from the doorway.

I looked up at her, surprised. "I'm taking care of it," I said. "Don't worry. I'm good with messages. If I concentrate, I can spell most of the words."

Heather laughed. "I know that. I'm just curious. Who called?"

I read Henry Barker's name off the notepad.

"Mr. Barker?" Heather asked, sounding alarmed. "Was it about the park rest rooms?"

I shrugged. "It was about the park, but he didn't say anything about rest rooms. He said that the mayor was going to ask the city council to cancel the permit."

"Oh, no!" Heather cried. She looked scared to death. "He can't do that to us! This is terrible!"

Suddenly I remembered the day Mr. Callahan came

close to threatening Heather with the loss of the permit. I knew she wouldn't need reminding. I bet she was furious with herself for not warning Uncle Will. But what could he have done?

Heather grabbed the notepad and stared at it. "The park is where the Centennial celebration is supposed to be held! That's where the fireworks display will be, and we're using the bandstand for the entertainment. And we've already promised space for the food vendors, and the balloon and postcard people, and the games, and—"

"And I bet all the posters and notices and letters say that everything will be at the park," I said. "I see what you mean—this could be an awful mess. What do you suppose Uncle Will's going to do?"

Heather stared at me. "I can't believe it's happening! I have no idea what he'll do if he loses the permit."

"But there has to be another place," I said. "What about the college campus?"

"The Quad is too small, and it isn't arranged right," she said. "And the football field would be too hot. Will and the committee rejected those ideas a long time ago. The park across the street from the campus is the best place. It's the right size, and has trees for shade and grass to sit on if the temporary bleachers are full."

And then she sat down at the table and burst into tears. "All that work went for nothing!" she cried. "Now what are we going to do? I hate Mayor Callahan! You can bet he's laughing his head off this morning."

I turned away from her and rinsed plates in the sink. Did Toby know yet what his father was trying to do?

"Uncle Will will think of something," I said.

"And there's time to print up more posters and send out letters."

"But it costs so much!" Heather said. "We've already spent every cent we had for promotion."

"Maybe the city council will refuse to cancel the permit," I said. "It hasn't happened yet."

Heather wiped away her tears. "You're right. I'm panicking over nothing. Will can talk to the people on the city council—he's good at that sort of thing. He'll make them realize that we can't change everything now."

She went back to the den to finish her typing, and I cleaned the kitchen. I should have felt better about things. After all, Heather was right. Uncle Will would straighten everything out, and their plans wouldn't have to be changed.

And Toby and I could stay friends.

I started the dishwasher and gave the counter a last swipe with a paper towel. Of course we'd stay friends! Nothing our families did would change that.

But I knew better.

He hadn't been in touch with me since the day we went to the island for a picnic. I tried to convince myself that he was back at his father's farm, where there was no phone, working hard but still thinking about me. Maybe even half as much as I was thinking about him.

Uncle Will and Aunt Marsha came home, and Heather reported the bad news about the mayor's newest attempt to spoil the Centennial. While the three of them discussed the problem, I wandered out to the mailbox to see if Nick had written again.

Instead, I found a letter from Brady Harris. The sight of it made me feel guilty. He'd written me twice before, and I'd answered him. But I hadn't given him much thought since his last letter, and now I felt awful.

The letter didn't say much, just that his dad was taking him and his little sister to San Francisco for a few weeks to visit their aunt and uncle, and he'd write me from there. He said he hoped I was enjoying myself more than I'd thought I would. He enclosed a drawing that his little sister had made of her cat, Shasta.

I sat down on the top step and reread the letter. Brady sounded the way he always did—caring and nice and affectionate.

Would you be hurt if you knew about Toby and me? I wondered.

And what about Toby and me? Is anything going on that Brady would need to worry about, if I was more than just a friend to him?

I took the rest of the mail inside and gave it to Aunt Marsha. And then I went upstairs before I overheard anybody say anything awful about the Callahan family.

Chapter 7

Dear Nick: Did you know that there have to be a certain number of johns for every hundred people in a public place? P (for people) divided by J (for johns) equals GS (for Good Sanitation), or, in other words, P ÷ J had better = GS or the mayor will #!**!. I know you've been waiting all your life for this news bulletin. And here's another one that's even sillier. Everybody's brain has blown all its circuits because our equation isn't correct. We have P ÷ J = GS − 1. Yes, I know you see the problem exactly. For lack of a loo, the kingdom was lost.

> Witnessing history being made,
> Erin

Two days and two dozen arguments later, Uncle Will found out that he and the mayor would have to present their cases to the city council at the same time. A sort of dinosaur debate. The mayor promptly left town for an indefinite period (the coward!), so the permit problem couldn't be solved for the time being. There was nothing Uncle Will, Heather, and the rest of the committee could do but wait until His Honor decided to roll back into town.

"Rules are rules, I guess," Uncle Will said morosely over lunch one day. "But this is becoming an uphill fight."

"Whatever happened to the Golden Rule—the one

that says we shouldn't do anything to anybody that we wouldn't want done to ourselves?'' Heather grumbled. She stuck her fork into her tomato with such force that it popped open and splashed juice on the front of her white shirt. ''I mean it!'' she exclaimed. ''Whatever happened to people doing nice things instead of all this rotten stuff? How can we cancel the Centennial because we don't have enough *toilets?*''

I rolled my eyes. ''Most people think they're supposed to do rotten things to others before everybody else gets a chance to do rotten things first.''

Amelia pushed her plate aside and put her head down on her arms. ''Oh, please, Erin,'' she said, ''don't remind me about the real world today. I have to do something—but I don't know what—about my lazy, goof-off clowns, and most of my ideas are either illegal or tacky.''

''Tell me about the illegal ones,'' Heather said, with the most hopeful expression I'd seen on her face for days.

''I'd better not,'' Amelia said. ''Just trust me when I tell you that they involve public humiliation, pain, tears, and maybe a lot of blood.''

''Are you going to rehearse the little devils again this afternoon, Amelia?'' Aunt Marsha asked. She poured herself another glass of ice water and pushed the jug across the table to Uncle Will.

''No, Aunt Marsha, I thought I'd just sock them all and leave town,'' Amelia said sourly.

I couldn't help laughing. ''Hey, I'll come with you today, and if anybody gets out of line, I'll play vice principal, or maybe school guidance counselor.''

''Yuck!'' Amelia cried. ''That's not funny. Hey, why don't you take part in one of the acts and set a good example. That would be the best help you could give me, Erin.''

I got to my feet and began gathering up all the empty plates. "I'll be a clown on the same day the mayor learns to dance the Virginia reel."

"Then get out the costumes, Erin," Uncle Will said, laughing at me. "You're about to become a clown. I've heard rumors that when the mayor was your age, he and his best girl won every dance prize in the county."

I had a sudden flashback to the night I danced the reel with Toby—the way he grinned down at me when he held out his hands to me. How his arm felt around my waist. The impatient way he pushed back his hair.

Could his father ever have been a boy like that?

Never.

After lunch, Amelia and I went to Sandy Graham's house. My cousin was in a bad mood, complaining about her hair color again. The clown act rehearsals were held in Sandy's family room, and we were the first ones there. In fact, not even Sandy was there.

"I'm sorry about this," Mrs. Graham said. "She told me that she'd be right back, but she had a great idea for her character and had to run a quick errand. She saw a really horrible necklace for sale at the discount store—something with little faces painted on big beads. I believe she said they looked much like shrunken heads, and if she glued a bit of yarn on them, the effect would be utterly disgusting."

Amelia burst out laughing. "Perfect. Sandy's forgiven for being late, then. But where's everybody else?"

Mrs. Graham shrugged. "You'll have to be tougher on them, I think."

Sandy bolted through the door then, swinging a plastic sack around. "Hey, you're here, too, Erin.

Great! Wait until you see what I bought for fifty cents.''

She took out a long, hideous necklace made of some sort of dried seeds, big ones, all wrinkled and nasty. And each one had a face painted on it.

"I think that originally these were supposed to be happy faces," Sandy explained as she dropped the necklace over her head. "But something happened to the seeds—they dried up too much, I guess—and so now the faces look awful. Aren't they great? Won't they be the perfect finishing touch for Crudella's outfit?"

"They do look like shrunken heads," I said, fascinated. "Hey, let me glue the hair on them. I'd love to help out."

Sandy took off the necklace and handed it to me. "Mom will get you yarn or whatever you need out of her sewing room. Meanwhile, let's get started, Amelia. I want to try that part again where you get sick and I call Dr. Dork."

Amelia was wearing her most patient look. "But this time you can't laugh at your own lines. Try hard not to do that. Really try."

They started pulling bits and pieces of their costumes out of a big storage closet in the hall outside the family room door. Sandy, who was Crudella, yanked ugly green tights on over her shorts and slipped high-heeled shoes with platform soles on her feet. Then she wiggled into a tight orange dress, put on rhinestone glasses mended with a big chunk of tape, and opened up a broken black umbrella over her head.

Amelia, who played Mindy Brunch, slung a thick padded vest over her head and fastened it around her hips. Then she let an enormous dress drift over her head and shoulders. It seemed to have been made out

62

of some sort of splotchy red and blue curtain material.

"Those have got to be the ugliest curtains I ever saw," I said. "In case you hadn't noticed."

"My Aunt Beth found them in the dump," Sandy said. "Along with a red velvet bedspread and a framed sign that said, 'Lover.' "

"You made that up," Heather said, laughing. "It's disgusting! How do you think up stuff like that?"

"It's true!" Sandy said. "Ask my mother! Aunt Beth brought home the sign, too, but Mom made her stuff it in the bottom of the garbage can and scrub her hands with disinfectant."

"Aren't you afraid of catching something from the curtains?" I asked my cousin Amelia, who actually seemed to be admiring her reflection in the mirror inside the closet door.

"Sandy's mother boiled them," Amelia explained. "That's why the colors ran. The blobs are supposed to be red and blue flowers."

"And you think *I* dress funny," I muttered.

"I remember when you wore a sweater that said Prison Farm on it," Amelia said.

"Did she?" Sandy cried, laughing.

"Yes," Amelia said, and she sounded practically proud of me. "And she had a shirt that said, 'You're fat and your mother dresses you funny.' She drove her counselor crazy."

"I wish you went to our school," Sandy said dreamily. "You'd make the biggest hit. Among the kids, I mean."

"I've retired the sweater and shirt," I said, remembering how I'd resolved to try to be a little more cooperative at school. "I can send them to you, if you like."

"Oh, yes, do that," Sandy's mother said, and she sighed, smiled, and left the room.

I decided I'd better keep my clothes.

"So where is everybody?" I asked, to change the subject. "What are they doing today instead of playing clown?"

"They are playing with fire," Amelia said, and she quit smiling. "Sandy, this dawdling around has got to stop. I mean it. After this, everybody turns up on time or I'm canceling the whole thing."

I could hear dogs barking in the street outside the house, and just then the back door to the family room burst open and Rod rushed in. He was wearing several yards of fake leopard skin draped around himself—over what seemed to be long underwear—and on his head was a silver helmet that emitted animal roars.

"This is Lionrump, the wild animal trainer," Sandy told me crossly. "And I can see that he just had to do his stupid thing again. He had to come over here all dressed up and making weird noises and setting off burglar alarms all over town."

"Hey, Erin," Rod said, ignoring her completely. "Great to see you. You wouldn't want to be a gorilla in the clown act, would you? I've got the costume, but nobody wants to help me out and wear it."

"Count me out," I said, just as the door opened again and Colin came in, carrying a shopping bag.

"Your stupid helmet opened our automatic garage door again," he told Rod. "If you're going to run all over the neighborhood with it, don't come down my street. And turn off the racket, for Pete's sake!"

Rod reached up to his helmet and flipped a small switch. The roars stopped.

"Where did you get that?" I asked. A million possibilities for its use paraded through my mind. Good old Nick would go crazy over it.

Rod tugged off the helmet. "It belongs to my little brother. It's part of his space suit outfit. There's a tape of rocket blast-off noises that goes with it. I put in the animal noises tape instead."

"Save your batteries for the Centennial," Amelia grouched. "Does anybody know where Paige and Thad are?"

"Thad's bringing over a big rubber drain stop to attach to my rubber tubing so I can have a stethoscope," Colin explained. "Dr. Dork needs more medical equipment."

"Is Thad bringing this drain stop all the way from Brazil?" Amelia asked.

I could see that she was losing her temper, but Colin didn't pick up on it. He thought she was trying to be funny.

"Not Brazil," he said. "They were all out. He got it at Berkley's Hardware over on Pine Street."

Paige rushed in then, with apologies and a bag of cookies. "Sorry, sorry," she said.

Amelia gave me a look that said, "See what I have to put up with?"

I got up and started for the door. "I'd better clear out of the way so you guys can rehearse. I'll take the necklace with me and fix it up at home. I'm sure I can get everything I need from Aunt Marsha."

At the door, I paused and turned around. "Listen, people," I said, "Amelia's really good at what she does. Too bad the rest of you find it so easy to take advantage of her." I grinned. "No insult intended, of course," I went on. "At least, not a really big one."

And with that, I left. I hoped what I said did some good.

When I reached the sidewalk, I saw Thad jogging toward me, carrying a small sack.

"You're late, and Amelia's upset," I said.

He stopped, embarrassed. "I know. I meant to be here an hour ago. We get worse every day."

"Maybe you should get better every day," I said, and I scowled. Nothing I did mattered much, since I'd be leaving town before long. But I was feeling sorry for my cousin.

He flushed, said, "Right," and ran past me toward the back of the house.

I marched on, full of righteous anger on Amelia's behalf. She was trying to do something nice for Heather, who was trying to do something nice for her stepfather, who was trying to do something nice for the whole town. But the whole dumb town seemed to be more interested in hanging around—or bickering—than getting things done.

If anybody had been interested in my advice—and I didn't think that it was too likely—I would have told my cousins to forget the Centennial and go someplace and have fun.

I strolled uptown, saw Uncle Will across the street talking to a few people, and decided to cross over and find out what was going on. He looked more than a little exasperated.

". . . and I expected more support from you folks," he was saying.

The taller of the two men shrugged, and the other said, "It's not as if we hadn't tried to talk sense into the mayor. He was against using the park from the beginning."

"We did our best to persuade him, Will," one of the women said. "But now he's out of town, and we have to wait until he gets back. Nobody can do anything until he's here; you know that. The council has dug in on this one. There's no point in making more enemies.''

I said hello and good-bye, and walked on. Hopeless. Grown-ups quarrel as much as kids do, and their disagreements are every bit as stupid. No, maybe even more stupid. Sometimes they end up going to war.

The war of the johns, I thought, and I burst out laughing.

I bought some chocolate-covered orange sticks in the candy store to cheer up my cousins, and started home. I was across from the library when I saw Toby, running down the steps with a book under his arm.

He saw me. I was sure he saw me. But he didn't wave until I shouted his name.

And he didn't stop, either.

I swallowed hard and kept going. Oh, I could act as if I didn't care. And why should I? I barely knew him. I'd be leaving this town in a few weeks, and maybe I'd never be back. So what difference did it make? Who cares? In a million years, nobody will know the difference.

I'd come all those miles to this silly little town that couldn't even have a Centennial celebration without raising enough fuss to make itself ridiculous! My cousins were working themselves to death for nothing. And I'd met a quiet boy who could dance an old-fashioned dumb dance and make it romantic and exciting. And we'd gone on a picnic. A picnic, believe it or not!

I, Erin Whitney, had been daydreaming about a country boy who'd spent only a few hours with me. Who obviously preferred not seeing me again. Whose father was less fun than a dog bite.

I would have given anything to hear him say my name one more time.

Chapter 8

On the following Sunday morning, shortly after
dawn, a summer storm broke. It was the worst one
I'd ever seen, with winds so fierce that the poplar
trees edging the street bent sideways and the air was
filled with green leaves torn loose.

I was expecting the house to be crushed any moment by a falling tree, so I scuttled out of bed, woke
Amelia (how could she sleep through that racket?),
and we hurried downstairs.

Uncle Will was making coffee. "I've lived here for
years," he said, "but I never get used to the storms
that come down off the mountains."

"Bear doesn't seem to mind the noise," I said,
poking the sleeping dog with one bare foot.

"Nothing bothers her," Uncle Will said. "Except
an empty food pan."

"Let's make scrambled eggs, bacon, and toast,"
Amelia said. "This isn't the sort of morning for a
summer breakfast of fruit and yogurt."

Uncle Will and I exchanged a look. "I can't ever face up to yogurt in the morning," he said. "That's the time of day when I wonder if I'm consuming an intelligence greater than my own."

"Oh, yuck!" Amelia cried. "That's horrible. Why did you tell me that? I'll think about it every time I eat yogurt now."

Uncle Will was smiling, but his back was turned to Amelia so she couldn't see, and I wasn't sure if she knew he was teasing her.

"Don't listen to Will when he's discussing food," Heather said from the doorway. She sounded grumpy. "He disgusted everybody a few months ago when he told us why you shouldn't eat raw fish."

"Why not?" I asked. I didn't eat raw fish, but I was curious.

"If he tells that story about parasites again, I'm moving out to the garage." Aunt Marsha shuffled into the kitchen, wearing fuzzy slippers and a heavy robe. "Isn't this a horrible morning? It isn't cold exactly, but I feel like January."

"The storms don't last long," Uncle Will told me. "Then the sun comes out and the mountains look so innocent that you'd never believe they could roll winds like this down on us."

"Will the poet," Heather grumbled. "I'm going straight to the den after breakfast and read the comics and watch cartoons."

It ended up that we all carried our plates to the den, with an interested Bear lumbering along behind, and watched Sunday morning cartoons while the wind howled around the house. And then, as suddenly as the storm began, it ended.

I watched at the window while the sun broke through the black, rolling clouds. Everything outside glittered and shone.

"Let's go for a walk," I said.

"You girls go," Aunt Marsha said. "Will and I planned on driving to Abbey Falls for the antique show."

"Let's go biking," Heather said to Amelia and me. "Mom and Will have bikes you two can use. We'll take lunch with us."

"But I've got stacks of work—" Heather began.

"Not today," Uncle Will said. "Go with your cousins, and don't even think about the Centennial."

"But I'm worried—" Heather began again.

"I can worry for both of us," Uncle Will said. "Go. Fix yourselves a big lunch, and be sure to take all the yogurt. It hasn't had any exercise—"

"Stop it!" Heather shouted, laughing. "You're making me feel so guilty that I'll end up buying a sympathy card for every carton I eat."

I did my best to laugh along with the others, but I couldn't seem to appreciate the family sense of humor that morning. The storm had suited my mood more than the sunlight afterward. Try as I might, I couldn't forget the way Toby had waved at me and walked off the afternoon before. He'd seemed so indifferent.

Well, I'd made an idiot out of myself, that was certain. Here I'd been thinking all along that he was feeling everything I was feeling.

No. I'd only been hoping it.

I shook my head to clear my thoughts. Dumb Erin. Hadn't I learned a long time before that you can't trust anybody?

It wasn't his fault that he didn't care about me, I thought. It was all mine. After all, just take a good look at me. My clothes and my weird hats came from First Pick, a used-clothing store in Seattle. My hair hadn't been cut since I was ten, when my parents were killed in an accident. I was rude on purpose,

70

whenever I could get away with it—and a lot of times when I knew I couldn't get away with it. The only boyfriend I'd ever had was Brady Harris, and he wasn't exactly a boyfriend. It was more of a mutual sympathy relationship—his mother was dead, too.

The truth was that I really didn't know how to act around a boy. I had turned Toby off someway, and I was too stupid to figure out how. And too proud to tell my cousins and ask for help.

"So where shall we go?" Heather asked, interrupting my private misery. "There are some good roads west of town."

"Let's go to Lost Lake," I said, suddenly anxious to stop myself from being so sentimental about the afternoon I'd shared with Toby.

"I don't know the way," Heather said. "Oh, that's where you went with Toby! Do you think you can find it again?"

Find it? I had memorized every inch of the way, and in my memories, I had traveled it over and over. "Sure," I said, trying to sound casual. "Let's leave around eleven. We'll have lunch on the island in the middle of the lake."

"Oh, that sounds romantic," Amelia said. "Is that where you and Toby had your picnic?"

"Yes," I said. I got up suddenly and started for the door. "I'll get dressed and make the beds, Amelia."

I had to get out of the den before they asked me any more questions about the picnic.

We left the house soon after eleven, and rode out the rain-washed roads toward Lost Lake. We didn't see many people, and I was glad for that. Heather had a tendency to stop and talk to everybody she knew or even thought she knew.

71

But then, Toby had stopped to talk with people several times that day, hadn't he?

Stop thinking about him, Erin!

While my cousins discussed their hair and how much they wanted to be blond, I did my best to pay attention. It wasn't easy.

The parking area beside Lost Lake was empty when we got there. But signs of the storm were everywhere. Two trees beside the lake had fallen, and a third sagged over the footbridge.

"We're lucky it didn't fall on the bridge," I told my cousins. "That's the only way to the island."

"Maybe we shouldn't cross it," Amelia said. "What if the tree falls and hits us when we're on the bridge?"

"If it didn't fall during the storm, it won't fall now," Heather said. "Somebody will have to come out and cut it down, though. It'll drop for sure in the next storm."

Amelia was still worried about the tree, so Heather crossed the bridge first, ducking under a low-hanging branch.

"See? It's safe enough," she called out from the island.

Amelia scuttled across, quick as a scared cat. "It's okay, Erin," she shouted.

I wasn't as afraid as Amelia, but I wasn't about to let on that I wasn't as brave as Heather, either. "Here I come," I said.

The bridge seemed as solid as it had before. Or rather, it didn't seem any more wobbly than it had before. When I reached the place where the tree hung down too low, I ducked as the others had. And just then I heard an ominous cracking sound.

"Run, Erin!" Amelia screamed. "The tree's coming down!"

I ran crouched over, so scared that I couldn't even yell. And the instant I reached the end of the bridge, the tree fell. The planks under my feet slanted suddenly. I leaped forward and fell awkwardly on land.

And then I looked back and saw the bridge disappear underwater, weighted down by the thick trunk and a tangle of branches.

"Are you all right?" Amelia asked me.

I nodded, but my heart was thudding under my ribs. Pain shot across my lower back and down my left leg. I rested my weight on my right leg and rubbed my left hip.

"You're hurt," Amelia said.

"Not really," I said. "I'll be okay in a minute. I just need to sit down." I hobbled over to one of the picnic tables and eased myself down on a bench.

"You could have been killed," Heather said.

"A miss is as good as a mile," I said, my voice shaking. I didn't need any reminding of my close call.

"So what do we do now?" Heather asked. "How do we get off this island?"

I looked across to the parking lot. It seemed farther away now than it had when I'd been here with Toby. But it still wasn't all that far. Not an impossible distance.

"When we're ready to leave, we'll just swim across," I said. "No big deal."

Neither of my cousins said a word. I looked up at them. "So we'll be a little wet," I said. "The sun's out. We'll dry off riding home on the bikes."

"Maybe you will," Heather said. "Amelia and I can't swim."

I gawked at them. "What do you mean, you can't swim? My grandmother taught me years ago! You're from Seattle. It's surrounded by water. How could you get to be this old and not know how to swim?"

"I don't know, Erin!" Amelia shouted. "We managed it, that's all. Some people like to swim, and other people don't."

"You own a dozen swimsuits!" I shouted back. "I've seen them. What do you do in them if you don't swim?"

"Get a tan!" Amelia shrieked. "Will you get off my case, Erin? I suppose you can swim ten miles, but I don't want to hear about it right now. Is there another way off this island or isn't there?"

I ground my teeth. "There isn't. That was the only bridge. Now are you satisfied?"

Amelia sat down across from me. "Great. Now what do we do?"

"Walk around the island and see if anybody else is here," I said. "If other people are here, they're stuck, too. At least the ones who can't swim are stuck. Maybe they have an idea."

I got up and marched away down the path without looking back to see if my cousins were following. My back didn't hurt as much as I thought it might, not at first. And even if it had, I wasn't about to let my cousins see that I wasn't perfectly all right. I had already figured out how this day was going to end. One way or another, I'd swim to shore and get help from somebody with a rowboat.

There was only one small problem with that idea. Yes, I certainly could swim—but only a short distance, and with much splashing and hard breathing. The awful truth was that none of the Whitney girls was much of an athlete.

I kicked a rock hard, hurt my back again, and kept going.

"Hey, is anybody here?" I shouted when I got to what I figured was the center of the island.

A few birds answered, but they weren't likely to be much help.

I called out a few more times, then marched on to the far side of the island, the place where Toby and I had stood when he showed me his father's farm. Maybe somebody would be there. Maybe even Toby himself.

The farm seemed deserted.

"Hey, is anybody over there?" I shouted. "Hey!"

No one answered.

I sat down on a log. The shore was farther away here than on the other side of the island. If I was going to swim, it would have to be from the other side. And then I had no idea how far I'd have to bike to reach a house.

"Might as well start now," I muttered to myself, and I tried to get up.

White-hot pain shot down my left leg, from my back to my heel. I gasped and would have sat down again, but that might have hurt even more.

I stood there on one leg for what seemed like an hour. Finally I had to force myself to walk, and I did, painfully, one dragging step at a time, until I reached the picnic area again.

My rotten, selfish cousins were lying flat on their benches, sunning themselves.

"You two make me so mad!" I yelled. "You're waiting for me to rescue you, and you aren't helping me at all! I ought to swim to shore and leave you here!"

They both shot to their feet, guilty as thieves. I hobbled toward them, angry enough to knock their heads together.

"You *are* hurt!" Amelia said. "I knew you were."

"Then why did you let me go off by myself?" I roared.

"Because you are so bossy, that's why!" she roared back.

"Both of you shut up, right this minute!" Heather howled. "How are we going to get out of this if Erin's hurt? Now none of us can swim, and Erin needs help. Quit yelling at each other and think."

"Let's get Erin up on a table so she can lie down," Amelia said.

But that was impossible. Even with them supporting me, I couldn't manage to step up on a bench. My back hurt worse every minute, and it took all my courage to keep from crying.

"The ground is wet," Amelia said. "She can't lie down there."

"I don't care how wet it is," I groaned. "Help me lie down."

"There's a plastic trash bag in the lunch box," Heather said. "We can tear it open—"

"We left the lunch with the bikes," Amelia said.

"Please tell me that we aren't going to be a twentieth-century version of the Donner party," I moaned.

Both of them screamed with laughter then, and I had to smile a little myself. "Actually, neither one of you looks good enough to eat," I said. "Come on, help me lie down, and then we'll make a plan."

They ended up spreading their sweaters on the ground, and I made myself as comfortable as I could. They sat on the bench, and we began waiting. And waiting.

"Somebody has got to drive down that road sooner or later," Heather said.

"Somebody will want to have a picnic on the island," I said. "I saw people the day Toby and I were here."

"The big storm probably changed most people's minds about having a picnic today," Amelia said.

"A delivery truck will come along. Or a mailman," Heather said.

"It's Sunday," I reminded her. Overhead, white clouds formed and re-formed in the bright sky. If I concentrated on them, my back didn't hurt so much.

The sun moved, bit by bit, across the sky. Sometimes my cousins and I talked. Other times we were silent, listening to the birds in the woods. Not a car passed on the road. No one came by on a bike.

My watch said three-fifteen when, at last, I heard a car in the distance. Forgetting my back, I tried to sit up. "Ow. Listen. I hear a car coming."

"I heard it, too." Heather jumped to her feet and ran to the water's edge.

"Get ready to yell," Amelia told her. "They might not look over here."

"I'm ready to *scream,*" Heather assured her.

The car came in sight, and both my cousins shouted at the top of their lungs. Miraculously, the car slowed, and then turned in to the parking lot.

"We're saved! We're saved!" Heather cried.

"For heaven's sake," Amelia complained. "You sound as if we're half-dead of exposure. Erin's the one who needs saving." But she was still waving her arms.

Heather kept up a steady shout. "Help us! We need help! We can't get off the island! Somebody's hurt! Help us!"

The car sat there. A man was inside, and he stayed behind the wheel. He didn't get out. He was only watching us. *Watching,* not helping.

And then the car moved slowly back toward the road.

"He's leaving! He can't do that!" Amelia screamed.

"Oh, yes he can," Heather said, angry. "Oh, yes. I recognize the car now. That was Mayor Callahan, and you can bet your life he can go off and leave us. It won't bother him a bit."

I shut my eyes. I couldn't believe this was happening.

"But you told him somebody was hurt!" Amelia exclaimed, and she sounded as if she couldn't believe what was happening either.

"He recognized me, I suppose," Heather said. "I really hate him, worse than ever now."

"But nobody would leave behind somebody who's hurt," Amelia cried. "Maybe he thought you were only kidding around."

"Sure, that's it," Heather said suddenly. She turned to me. "This is all my fault, Erin. He can't stand me, and I suppose he thought I was pulling off some sort of practical joke."

But I read her face, and I knew that she was lying. Mayor Callahan went off and left us because that's the sort of person he was.

Toby's father.

I turned my head and burst into tears.

The day went on and on. My cousins invented a dozen plans to get us off the island, but none of them were workable. Some of them made me laugh, especially the one involving them finding a log that would float, putting me on it, and setting me adrift in the lake with the hope that I'd wash ashore on the other side.

"Let's face it," I told them in late afternoon. "We're going to have to wait until Aunt Marsha and Uncle Will start worrying about us and send out search parties."

"It could be dark by the time anyone finds us," Heather said.

"It could be tomorrow," Amelia said.

"Look on it as an adventure," I said. "That's what I'm trying to do."

"Adventure!" Heather cried. "All I can think about is that rotten man driving back to town and not saying anything to anybody about our being here."

"I thought he was out of town and couldn't be reached," Amelia said. "Isn't that why Uncle Will couldn't talk to the city council about using the park?"

"Well, the big jerk was out of town," Heather said. "Obviously he was hiding out somewhere around here."

"On his farm," I said. "He owns a farm on the other side of the lake. Toby works there. And so does a handyman. But nobody seemed to be around when I yelled across the lake earlier."

"Mayor Callahan was," Heather said. Her hands were clenched into fists. "I bet he heard you."

"Maybe not," I said. "The bunkhouse where Toby stays is so far away that you can't even see it from the island."

"Well, we'll have time to think up a way to get even," Amelia said with what sounded like diabolical satisfaction.

"Just give me a chance," Heather said. "I'm thinking about things involving chains and hot coals."

The day went on. The sun sank behind the trees, and I began feeling cold. But I didn't complain. My cousins felt bad enough. And my back didn't hurt if I lay still. Not much, anyway.

I think we were all half-asleep when I heard the sound first. Hundreds of bird voices trilled all at once, fell silent, and then trilled again.

"Listen!" I said. "Toby's here."

"What?" Heather mumbled. "What are you talking about? Nobody's here but us."

"Not here, I mean on the farm. Toby's on the farm, and he's shaking the wind chimes so the birds will sing."

The birds trilled again, paused, trilled, paused, and then broke into wild song.

Heather was on her feet. "Which way shall I go? Will I be able to see him? Can he hear me if I yell?"

"Follow the path," I said. "Go clear across the island. You'll see the farm. Start calling him right away. He'll be listening for the birds, and so he'll be sure to hear you."

I hoped.

Heather took off and disappeared into the shadowy woods. Amelia sat down beside me and grabbed my hand.

"He'll help us," she said. "He can't be like his rotten father. He'll phone Uncle Will . . ."

"There's no phone at the farm," I said. "But Toby has a canoe, and he can get us off the island."

We could hear Heather shouting Toby's name, over and over. The birds went crazy with the racket she was raising. One way or another, Toby would know something strange was happening on the island.

It didn't take as long as I thought it would. Heather rushed back to tell us that Toby had heard her and was bringing the canoe around to our side of the island.

"He'll be here right away, Erin," she said. "He promised."

It was nearly dark then. Amelia helped me sit up, and I was the first one to hear the paddle in the lake.

"Here he is," Amelia said.

Here he is, I thought. Here he is. The pain in my back was like a wild thing biting me, and I hated

80

having him see me like this, with my eyes swollen with tears.

He knelt beside me. "Hey," he said. "I know you didn't like the bridge, but did you have to knock it down?"

In spite of everything, I laughed, and without thinking, I reached out to him.

He wrapped his arms around me and whispered, "I'll take you home."

Chapter 9

Dear Nick: No, I won't tell you what's wrong. Not yet.

Erin

I can't remember much about the next few hours, because my back hurt so bad that I couldn't think about anything else. But there's one thing I'll remember—until I die. Toby and I were in the canoe. I was lying almost flat, with my head resting on my cousin's rolled-up sweaters. Suddenly he stopped paddling, bent over me, and brushed his hand over my forehead.

"You can cry if you want to," he said. "I'll never tell anybody."

"I'm doing fine," I said. "Honestly."

"I'm not," he said. "You're breaking my heart. I was already . . ."

"Already what?" I asked.

He was silent for five heartbeats. Then he said, "I was already thinking about you too much."

I looked up, past his face, to where the stars hung in the dark blue sky.

"Toby," I said, "look up at the stars now, so that we can both see them at the same time."

He tipped his head back, and after a moment he laughed a little, but it wasn't a very happy sound. "Should we make a wish?"

"I don't think it would do any good," I said. My tears blurred the stars. "Toby?"

He looked down at me. "What?"

"You didn't think about me *too* much."

After that, everything got pretty hazy. I would have been scared if I'd been with anybody else.

I barely remember what comes next. According to my cousins, Toby left me lying on the grass at the edge of the parking lot, rushed off to call an ambulance, then paddled the canoe back to the island for Amelia and Heather. Within an hour, I was in the small Fox Crossing Hospital, with Uncle Will and Aunt Marsha leaning over my bed.

During that night several strangers examined me, X-rayed me, questioned me, and one of them, a doctor with a short white beard, actually pricked my legs with a pin and laughed when I yelled, "Quit that! It hurts!"

"Trust me, you're lucky you feel it," he said. "And furthermore, in my expert opinion, anybody who can yell that loud will live to be at least a hundred."

"No thanks to you," I grumbled. "When can I go home?"

"It's four o'clock in the morning," he said. "People who get me out of bed at this time don't deserve to go home for several days at least. Maybe not even until you're at least thirty-five years old, depending on how you behave."

"If you'd fix my back so it doesn't hurt, I'll go home right now," I said.

"Your back will fix itself, and soon, too, if you do as you're told. Lots of bed rest. No aggravation. And stay out from under falling trees." He wrote several things on my chart and started toward the door. "I sent your boyfriend home," he said. "If there's anything I can't stand, it's seeing some young buck mooning around the halls and pestering the nurses for bulletins on the state of his ladylove's health.''

He was talking about Toby. About the only thing I could do that didn't hurt was smile, and so I smiled.

''Bosh,'' the doctor said, seeing my face. ''I hate young love. All that blushing and giggling and hanging around looking hopeless and helpless. Outrageous. He'd better stay away from you.'' And then he left.

But Toby didn't stay away. I was in the hospital, most of the time flat on my back, for four days. And every night, just before the end of visiting hours, Toby slipped into my room and sat down on the chair next to my bed.

''Hello,'' he'd always say, soberly, his voice so quiet that I could hardly hear him. ''How was your day?''

Only a million years long, I'd think, because I've been waiting for you.

''Fine,'' I'd say. ''I'm getting better fast.''

Each night he brought me a small pink rosebud, one that didn't have thorns on the stem. They grew at the farm, he told me. For Toby, everything wonderful was at the farm. For me, everything wonderful was sitting beside my bed.

We never talked about his father. I didn't tell him that the mayor could have rescued me hours earlier than Toby had, but I was certain that Toby heard about it. My cousins were making sure that everybody in town knew all the details. Heather and Paige wanted to put up posters all over Fox Crossing, denouncing the mayor as a coward and a monster, and it took all my persuasive powers (I said I'd sock them good and hard) to forget that idea.

My Uncle Jock and Aunt Ellen, in Oklahoma for the family reunion, phoned the hospital and Will over and over, wanting to know if they should fly home and drive to Fox Crossing to check on me. It was only when I spoke to them and told them that I was fine, better than fine, ready to take on anybody who argued with me, that they finally seemed to quit worrying.

On the afternoon before I went home, during Uncle Will's usual second visit of the day, he said, "I had it out with Mayor Callahan this morning."

"About the permit to use the park?" I asked.

"About you," Uncle Will said. "I told him that I knew what he'd done—that he could have helped you, but chose instead to leave you there to suffer."

I grinned. "So did he give you the permit after you finished with him?"

Uncle Will shook his head. "The Centennial wasn't part of that conversation. I was talking about simple human decency."

"Oh," I said. "Then he didn't get the point, did he?"

Uncle Will laughed. "How come you're so smart?"

"Because I've known lots of Mayor Callahans," I said.

Uncle Will slumped a little in the chair. "I wish I could say that he sent along his apologies to you, and his best wishes for your recovery. But he denied knowing that anyone had been hurt, and then he blamed Heather for having a reputation as a prankster. That, of course, is true. She's a lively girl. But I have no doubt that he knew she wasn't joking."

"I hope he isn't taking this out on Toby," I said.

"It occurred to me that he might come down hard on his son," Uncle Will said. "So I took great pleasure in calling the newspaper to tell them how young

Toby Callahan rescued my niece. Toby will be on the front page. I don't think his father would dare start anything now.''

"Thanks," I said. "I've been worried about that. But what's happening with the Centennial? I ask Heather, but she only says that everything's working out."

Uncle Will shrugged. "There isn't much time left, so it looks like the athletic field will be our answer. Then we'll pray for cool, cloudy weather, but no rain. I'm afraid our usual scorching August sun would send the visitors running for the nearest campground in the forest."

I thought of Amelia's heavy, padded clown costume. In the sun, she'd be miserable. In the rain, she'd be too water-logged to move. "I'll keep my fingers crossed for cloudy, dry weather," I told Uncle Will.

The next afternoon, my last in the hospital, Amelia's clown troupe paid me a visit in costume. They even put on a small part of their act in the sun-room. The improvement in their performance was so amazing that I could hardly believe it.

At least something had turned out right.

My back didn't hurt much anymore, unless I did something wild like trying to climb stairs. So Aunt Marsha and Uncle Will borrowed a cot and set it up in the living room for me, and as soon as I got home, I lay down on it and heaved a big sigh.

"I feel really stupid," I said. "I hope I'll be able to get up and down stairs pretty soon. If I don't, you guys are going to be sick of having me in your way."

"It's not as if you have to spend all day lying down," Aunt Marsha said. "But you'll need to go to bed early, and of course, no more long bike rides for a while.''

The only long bike ride I wanted to take was with Toby, and I didn't need to hear out loud that I couldn't go again very soon. I wasn't even sure if I'd see him unless we arranged to meet somewhere away from the house. Toby didn't seem too anxious to run into my family, and I could understand that. They didn't blame him for what his father had done, but he couldn't be expected to understand that.

But later that evening, at his usual time, Toby showed up at the door with a pink rose.

I'd been lying on the cot propped up with pillows and watching an old TV movie, with Bear for company. The dog had decided that having me sleep in the living room was the best idea since automatic dog feeders—because as soon as everybody else left the room, she always jumped up on the couch, and she knew I couldn't make her get down. When Aunt Marsha showed Toby in to the living room, Bear slid to the floor and stayed there just long enough for Aunt Marsha to leave the room. Then, before Toby could sit down on the couch, Bear jumped back up on it.

''It's really hopeless,'' I said, laughing. ''She won't mind anybody except Uncle Will and Aunt Marsha, and then only if they're looking straight at her.''

''She's just like her sister,'' Toby said, studying Bear, who pretended she didn't know he was standing over her. ''Heidi oozes up on the couch every time Thad turns his back.''

''Oozes,'' I said. ''That describes it exactly. Usually Bear's so clunky that I wonder how she manages to get around without hurting herself. But when it comes to getting up on the furniture, she's as limber as a snake.''

Toby handed me the rose and pulled a chair close

to the side of the cot. "You look like you're feeling better," he said.

"I'll be good as new tomorrow," I said. I was hoping that he'd ask me to meet him somewhere—in the park or the college campus. Someplace where we could talk.

But Toby changed the subject. "It's been awfully hot these last few days. Some of the kids have been rafting on the river. You ought to see them. Most of the rafts are homemade, and they usually fall apart almost as soon as they hit the water. Everybody would drown if the river weren't so shallow in August."

"Do you take your canoe out on the river?" I asked.

"I would, with you," he said. "But it's more fun with a raft. Or even an inner tube or an air mattress. I wanted to take you, but now I guess you can't go."

"No," I said, practically grinding my teeth in frustration. "At least, not this week." Or for the rest of the summer, I thought, remembering the doctor's nagging.

Would there be another time, another summer? He didn't ask, but only sat there, playing with the end of my braid, brushing the end across the back of his hand.

"Did you see the paper?" I asked, to break the painful silence.

He looked up. "Did you?"

"Uncle Will showed it to me as soon as I got home," I said. "That was a nice picture of you."

"Thad gave it to the reporter," Toby said. He seemed embarrassed. "There should have been a picture of you."

"I wasn't the hero, you were," I said.

He looked away from me. I could read his mind—he was thinking about his father. "The article said you still planned on staying here until the end of August.''

''Yes,'' I said. There's plenty of time for us, I thought.

No, there isn't, I told myself. There could never be enough time.

He wrapped my braid around his hand and tugged gently. ''Rapunzel,'' he said. ''Remember the fairy tale? I couldn't remember her name at first, so I went the library and found the story in the children's section.'' He grinned. ''You aren't anything like her, you know. I can't imagine you putting up with being a prisoner in a tower.''

''No,'' I said. Inside, I was dismayed. Is that what he wanted? A girl who waited to be rescued? I'd been rescued from the island only because I couldn't help myself.

''You're the one who's locked in the tower,'' I blurted.

He understood me completely. ''I get free every September when I go away to school,'' he said.

For a moment, I thought he was going to say something more, but he didn't. Instead, he let go of my braid and stood up.

''It's not late,'' I said, protesting.

''You must be tired.'' He grinned, but I didn't think he was happy. ''I'm going back out to the farm tomorrow morning.''

''Then I won't see you for a while,'' I said.

He only looked at me. Finally he said, ''Take care of yourself,'' and he left.

I blinked hard until I was sure I wouldn't cry, because I knew that the second Heather and Amelia heard the front door close, they'd rush in and question me.

"He's crazy about you," Amelia said as she skidded in.

"He's gorgeous!" Heather shouted.

Aunt Marsha followed them. "Romeo and Juliet," she said, and she wasn't smiling. "Be careful, Erin."

I looked over at Uncle Will, who was standing in the doorway. "Well?" I asked. "Let's hear your opinion."

He regarded me thoughtfully. "Shakespeare said, 'Lest too light winning . . .' "

" 'Make the prize light,' " I finished, and I grinned at him.

"What does that mean?" Heather demanded.

"It means that Erin's so calm about all this that she can still show off how much she reads," Amelia said.

"It means that anything that comes too easily probably isn't worth having," I said, and I settled myself down in my pillows, yawning, prepared to sleep. I don't know why, but I felt better.

The others took the hint, even Bear, and everybody left the living room. Aunt Marsha switched off the light.

A few minutes later, when I was nearly asleep, I heard a horrendous yelp from the kitchen and much shouting from my cousins.

"What's happening?" I called out, but nobody answered me.

I couldn't stand not knowing what had gone wrong, so I eased myself out of bed (oozed, Toby would have said) and hurried to the kitchen.

Poor Bear was sitting in the middle of the floor, holding up a front paw.

"She caught her paw in the pantry door," Heather explained.

"No, I was careless and I slammed her foot in the door," Amelia wept. "Look at it! It's bleeding."

Aunt Marsha was kneeling in front of Bear, examining the injury. "It's not much more than a nick," she said.

Bear groaned and rolled her eyes toward Amelia.

"This is terrible!" Amelia cried. "I practically killed her."

"I'm sure that she will recover completely if you administer a large dog treat," Uncle Will said.

Amelia practically tripped over her feet getting a treat out of the box on the counter. Bear crunched it and then looked around pathetically.

"Don't give her more," Aunt Marsha said. "Find that bottle of peroxide in the bathroom, Heather. And bring the box of cotton, too."

Heather, Amelia, and I exchanged panicked looks. The bottle was nearly empty after our attempt to bleach our hair. Would Aunt Marsha wonder what had happened to it?

But she only shook her head when Heather handed her the bottle, and said, "I should have picked more up. I didn't realize that we were nearly out."

She soaked a wad of cotton with peroxide and rubbed Bear's paw with it. Bear, interested, watched without a whimper.

"Won't that bleach her hair blond?" I asked, trying to pretend that it was an innocent question.

"No, this is medicinal-strength peroxide," Aunt Marsha said. "There you go, Bear. Your paw ought to be fine now."

She stood up and capped the bottle. "There's another kind of peroxide," she went on. "It's much stronger, and used in hair coloring."

"Oh," Heather said.

Aunt Marsha put the peroxide and cotton back in the bathroom. Uncle Will went upstairs with her a moment later, and my cousins and I stood gawking at one another in the kitchen.

"No, you don't," I said, before either of them could speak. "I'm definitely not up to mixing up another mess to put on your hair."

"Well, we wouldn't do it while you're still hurting," Amelia said.

"And we couldn't possibly do it until we made arrangements with Paige," Heather said.

"Maybe next week," Amelia said. "It's just that I'm so sick of my hair, and so is Heather, and we both would love a new look in time for the Centennial."

"And I've wanted to do something like that for a long time," Heather said. "And naturally Paige will want to change her hair at the same time. I can hardly wait."

"I'm going to bed," I said, and I limped back to the living room, with Bear lumbering close behind.

"They are crazy," I told Bear.

She slipped up on the couch, lay down, and sighed.

"They'll forget all about it," I said.

I had better things to think about than my cousins' hair color while I was drifting off to sleep. When Toby came back from the farm, he'd visit me. I was sure of it. Maybe we'd talk then, really talk.

Soon.

Chapter 10

Dear Nick: Thanks for the get-well cards and the coloring book. I'm feeling much better now. By the way, have I ever mentioned to you that I think adults are totally crazy? They do things that none of us would ever do.

> Color me disgusted,
> Erin

Uncle Will finally had his joint meeting with the mayor in front of the city council, although by that time we knew what the result would be. The mayor brought stacks of paper proving that every health ordinance in the entire universe would be violated when the Centennial visitors lined up all at one time to use the park johns (as if that were likely to happen).

I got the official news at the dinner table and demanded, "Who ever died from waiting in line for the john?"

"Only the ones who got murdered because they pushed in ahead of everybody else," Heather said. She grabbed another piece of bread and slapped butter on it. "All that work for nothing! I can't believe this has really happened. I kept telling myself that somehow it would all go away."

"Well, we can console ourselves that we have alternative plans," Uncle Will said. "Such as they are."

"We'd better get busy and start putting up signs directing people from the park to the campus," Heather said.

"And then we can put up arrows pointing to the athletic field," Amelia said.

Aunt Marsha refilled our water glasses. "There isn't time to send out letters, is there?"

"No time, no money," Uncle Will mourned.

"So people will leave their cars by the park, find out they have to move to the campus . . ." Aunt Marsha began.

"And get mad and go home," Heather finished. She shoved the last of her bread in her mouth and chewed savagely.

"No, they won't do that." Uncle Will obviously refused to be discouraged. "I wish there were a way to make it all seem part of our plan, though. As it is, we're going to sound unorganized."

"Only because we are," Heather said.

That evening, the Centennial committee had a meeting in the den, with Heather included. Amelia, Aunt Marsha, and I sat at the kitchen table lettering signs and cutting arrows out of red poster board.

"Does your back hurt?" Aunt Marsha asked for the tenth time.

"No," I said truthfully as I once more lettered "Meet us on the campus!" in red, waterproof paint on white cardboard.

We had a pile of signs saying, "Fox Crossing Centennial—follow the arrows." We had another pile that said, "This way to the Centennial."

"Now all we need is one big stake," I said.

"I thought you were going to nail these to trees," Aunt Marsha said.

"I meant a stake to drive through the mayor's heart," I said.

They laughed, and so did I, and for a moment I forgot that the mayor was Toby's dad. Incredible. They were so different.

He must be like his mother, I thought.

"What's Mrs. Callahan like?" I asked Aunt Marsha.

"I really don't know her," she said. "Quiet. Very pretty. I think I told you that she runs a dress shop."

"She sells fabulous clothes," Heather said. "We ought to go in there and look around. The mayor may be a jerk, but the rest of the family is pretty nice."

I let Heather's suggestion pass. But I liked the idea of dropping in the shop and seeing Mrs. Callahan for myself. Except that I wanted to do it alone.

The next morning, after Uncle Will left for another meeting and Aunt Marsha drove to the clinic, Heather and Amelia wanted to march off right away to put up the signs and arrows.

"After all," Heather grumbled as she stirred strawberries into her yogurt, "we might as well face facts. It's gotta be done."

"That's a big job for only the two of us," Amelia said. "Let's call up the clowns and make them help."

"Call up the clowns and tell them to get suited up and turn out for practice," I said. "They can clown around and put up signs at the same time—and look at all the attention they'll get. That will help the cause."

"And it will drive the mayor right out of his mind," Heather said, with satisfaction.

"We'll have a parade," Amelia said.

"Do you know kids who play band instruments?" I asked.

Heather stared at me. I could practically see the wheels in her head turning. "Yes!" she shouted. "Yes, yes, yes!"

She spent a busy half hour on the phone and then rushed back in the kitchen, babbling. "It's all set! I've got two trumpets, a trombone, a drummer, Rod's little sister who plays the flute, and somebody's uncle who wants to come along and play the bagpipes. Everybody's showing up at the park in an hour, and the clowns will be in costume, and Thad will push Erin in a wheelbarrow, and Dr. Dork will take care of her."

"No!" I shouted. "I'll walk."

"You can't," Heather said. "Wear the hat with the rose. It'll be perfect."

I drank the last of my orange juice, thought this over, and decided that it sounded like fun. At least, it sounded like a story I could repeat to Nick and get a big laugh.

"I'll get the hat," I said. "You get Thad and the wheelbarrow."

The wheelbarrow was huge, which was fine, because we needed room for me and the signs both. The clowns and musicians formed their parade at our house (pity the neighbors), and the parade headed toward the park.

Everywhere we went, we drew a crowd. It was terrific.

We took a detour down the street where the mayor's office was located. Thad made a big show of taking my pulse (he was wearing thick gardening gloves) and my temperature (with a long stick painted half red) in front of the mayor's windows. The bagpipe player honked an especially dismal rendition of "Danny Boy." Maybe we didn't actually see the mayor watching, but I was sure he was.

Part of me felt a little guilty for Toby's sake. But he was out at the farm and wouldn't see us.

And his father deserved it.

By the time we reached the park, we had a large following of laughing adults, yelling kids, barking dogs, and some puzzled Asian tourists who had stopped off in Fox Crossing on their way to Canada. A newspaper photographer took our picture while Thad was trying to bandage my left leg with a long strip of an old sheet. My right leg was already in a splint made out of a plastic hanger and several hundred feet of Christmas ribbon, complete with bows and a piece of plastic holly.

The crowd, except for the tourists, followed us to the campus. We made two trips around the beautiful Quad and stopped in front of the Fine Arts Building so that the piper could honk out his own version of the Fox Crossing College song. Some of the people in the crowd, obviously graduates, sang along. The overall effect was too horrible to describe, but the piper, who seemed to be well-known, got a big round of applause afterward.

Heather bent down and whispered, "Erin, you are a genius."

"Too true," I said.

"Genius, my foot," Amelia said. "Erin's just used to making great big public scenes, thank goodness!"

Everybody laughed, the piper tooted me some sort of salute, and we marched on (rode on, in my case) to the athletic field on the other side of the campus.

It was too hot to make more than one circle around the field. After that, we took refuge in the dusty shade behind the bleachers and rested for a while.

"The signs are all up," Amelia announced.

"Not that anybody in town is in doubt now about where the celebration will be held," Thad said.

"They heard us in Abbey Falls," Colin said.

"In Seattle," Paige announced. "I'm sure of it."

"But I'm going to hate doing our clown act here,"

Amelia said. She must have been cooking in her heavy costume. "The sun's a killer out on the field."

"You'll have to leave your padding home if it's hot that day," Paige advised.

"But that would ruin everything," Amelia said. "Nope, the show must go on, even if I die of sunstroke."

The piper told us to stay where we were, disappeared for a while with the wheelbarrow (after helping me out of it), and came back with a load of cold drinks and hamburgers.

"For the cause," he said.

We cheered him, and somebody more charitable than I asked him to play for us while we ate. Fortunately, he refused. He was, without a doubt, the worst piper I'd ever heard, but nobody could fault his enthusiasm.

It was the middle of the afternoon before I was finally wheeled home by the clowns. After everybody left, my cousins and I, with the dog, stretched out on the porch furniture in the shade and discussed our triumph.

"Everybody who comes can find the way to the Centennial now," Heather said contentedly.

"Right," Amelia said. "They'll know right where to go to see the clowns and the other acts and the food vendors and the souvenir people drop dead in the heat."

"Maybe it will be cool that day," I said.

"I'd better not hope too much for that," Heather said. "It's always better to plan for every disaster."

We thought that over for a while. Sometimes life is impossible.

"At least we'll be blondes by then," Amelia said, nodding emphatically.

Uncle Will came home only long enough to eat a

quick dinner, and then he ran off again for another meeting, this time with caterers. Aunt Marsha had an evening appointment with her hairdresser, so she left a few minutes after Uncle Will.

"Speaking of hairdressers," Heather said.

"I didn't know we were," I said, "and don't start up with the peroxide again."

"I'm wild to try it on my hair," Heather said.

"And it has to be a lot cheaper than those bleaching kits," Amelia said.

"Let's go for a walk to the drugstore and see what they've got," Heather said.

"Why don't the two of you set your hair on fire and get it over with," I said. "You're bound to look better than you will if you try fooling around with bottles of stuff you don't know anything about."

"*You* know about it," Heather declared. "You said you did."

"I told you everything I know. You mix the stuff with soap flakes, which don't exist anymore, I guess, and wait until your hair turns blond. If you trust your hair to that expert advice, then you are a lunatic. If I were you, I'd get out a carton of yogurt and ask its advice."

Heather glared at me. "I'm going to kill Will for getting you started on that yogurt business."

"Help, help!" I cried in a squeaky voice. "Heather's eating us! Help!"

Amelia howled with laughter. Bear raised her head, stared at us with the most offended expression, and dropped back to sleep again.

"Come on, let's go to the drugstore," Heather said. "Do you feel up to it, Erin?"

"Sure," I said. "I wouldn't miss this for anything. I also hope to be present when your parents ground you for the rest of your life because you turned your hair green.''

But Thad showed up then, and Heather wasn't about to share her plans with him, so the four of us sat outside until dark. Aunt Marsha was home by then, and Uncle Will returned a few minutes later, with ice cream and a box of late summer strawberries.

"Tomorrow," Heather whispered to me. "We'll go to the drugstore tomorrow."

"You'd better borrow one of Amelia's clown wigs," I warned her. "It'll be an improvement over what you'll look like if you go through with this."

"What are you two whispering about?" Thad asked.

"It's a surprise," Heather said.

"It'll be a surprise, all right," I told him, laughing.

She should have taken it seriously.

Chapter 11

Dear Nick: Thanks for sending the newspaper
clipping. Everybody here was happy that the
Centennial made news in Seattle. But we hated
seeing the mayor's picture with the article. I
can't believe that creep! He did everything he
could to ruin the celebration, and then he
sneaked off to Seattle to brag himself up and take
credit for all Uncle Will's hard work.

> Furious in Fox Crossing,
> Erin

The next morning, my cousins and I were the first
customers in the drugstore. I tried to steer them toward the hair-lightening kits, but they kept muttering
about how broke they were, and why spend more than
you have to in order to get the job done.

I picked up a bottle of industrial-strength peroxide
and read all of the fine print on the label. It did not
give instructions for bleaching hair.

"Obviously this stuff is for people who know what
they're doing," I said. "You don't, so don't buy it."

"*You* know what we're doing, and that's enough,"
Heather said. She dug through her coin purse and
handed Amelia some money. "Here, take this,
Amelia. Paige said she'd pay you for her share next
time she sees you."

"I refuse to have any part of this crazy business,"
I announced.

"When you see how great we look, you'll be sorry," Amelia said.

"When you get declared a disaster area, you'll wish you'd listened to me," I said. "I never should have told you what I'd read about peroxide. If it wasn't against my principles to fink on blood relatives, I'd run home and tell Aunt Marsha what you're planning."

"She wouldn't stop us," Heather said.

"So how come you didn't tell her at breakfast?" I demanded.

"Because she gives advice. You know, Mother-type advice. It always begins with 'When I was your age,' and ends with 'So try to learn something from my mistakes.' And then she lets me go and do whatever stupid thing I wanted to do anyway."

" 'Stupid' is the significant word here," I said. "Are you guys listening to yourselves talk, or are you just airing out your vocal cords?"

The clerks were watching us arguing among ourselves, and I began feeling conspicuous. "Let's get out of here."

"Not without this," Heather said, holding up the peroxide bottle.

Amelia paid for it at the checkout stand, and we left the store.

"Are you going to use that stuff today?" I asked.

"No time," Heather said. "As soon as I check on the signs in the park, I've got to rush home and take the Centennial dinner program to the printer's. We should have done it earlier—I don't know why Will's been putting it off. You'd think it was some sort of state secret. But it has to be taken in today, or I'll end up typing every single program myself."

"And I've got to rehearse the clowns again," Amelia said. "I thought we'd go through everything at the athletic field so we can see how things work. And how miserable we'll be while we're running around in the hot sun.''

We crossed the street to the park and started down the nearest path. Our signs looked good. I didn't see how anybody could get lost.

Under the trees, the grass was cool and smelled sweet. The bandstand faced out over a beautiful, shaded area that would have been a perfect place for an audience to sit and watch Amelia's clowns and all the other acts.

Well, I thought, no point in regretting what's no longer possible. But compared to the college athletic field, this place was paradise.

"Hey," Heather said. "Look who's coming."

I turned and saw Toby walking along the path we had just taken.

"I thought I saw the three of you ahead of me," he said.

He spoke to all of us, but he looked only at me.

"You're through working at the farm?" I asked.

"For now." He looked over at a sign Heather had nailed to a tree the day before. "I saw the arrows pointing toward the campus. Were the Whitney girls responsible for this?"

"We had a lot of help," Heather said, laughing. She told him about the clowns and musicians.

"It looks like you've solved the problem of where to hold the Centennial celebration," Toby said.

"More or less," Heather said. "The college athletic field is a poor second choice to this park. It's so hot and dusty. And the bleachers face south, so everybody will roast."

"But the fireworks will be at night," Toby said, sounding bewildered. "Won't you do everything else then, too?"

Heather explained about how all the musical and comedy acts would be running all day, and how the clowns would repeat their performances, too. "And then there are the vendors," she went on, "the people who sell souvenirs and food. They had counted on setting up under the trees at the edges of the park, where it's always cool."

"They could use pushcarts and circle around on the Quad," Toby said. "That's what they did during the big celebration when the college opened."

"How do you know what they did?" Heather asked.

"My dad's got a whole stack of scrapbooks," Toby said. "His family saved everything they could find about the opening, and I've looked through all of it. More than once. The vendors used pushcarts, and I remember one photograph of some singers standing on the steps of the Fine Arts Building with a lot of people watching them."

"You mean they used the steps of the buildings facing the Quad as open-air theaters?" Heather demanded.

Toby shrugged. "Something like that. Dad's got lots of photographs, and it looks as if people wandered around from one thing to another, and the vendors circulated between them, selling things."

Heather hugged herself. "Oh, boy, I can't believe I'm this lucky. We need to see all of those scrapbooks. Do you suppose you could let me borrow them? I bet we could get lots of ideas from them."

"And they'd be sort of traditional ideas, too," Amelia said. "People always like that."

"We could even see if the vendors would be interested in dressing the way people did then . . ." Heather began.

"Maybe we ought to find out what else the college

did," Amelia interrupted. "There could be all kinds of things we could do that nobody's thought of yet."

"Did they use the park?" Heather asked Toby.

He laughed. "The park didn't exist then. I think it was somebody's pasture."

"If they did it all without the park a hundred years ago, we can do it now," Heather said. "But we need the scrapbooks." She looked at Toby so confidently that I almost believed he'd be able to help.

He looked horribly embarrassed. "Dad keeps them in his office," he said. "I could ask, but . . ."

Heather winced. "He'd want to know why you wanted them, and there's no way he'd let me look at them."

"Sorry," Toby said. "I can try, but you'd better not count on it."

"Maybe we shouldn't involve Toby in this," I said suddenly.

"No, it's okay," Toby said.

Heather shook her head. "No, it's not. Sorry. I shouldn't have tried to put you in the middle. Look, I'll tell Will about this right away. There must be other photographs and records of the opening ceremony. We'll use those."

"The college must have something—maybe even more than the mayor," Amelia said.

"Come on, let's go find Will and get started with this," Heather said.

"I'll catch up to you later," I said, hoping my cousins understood that I wanted to be alone with Toby for a while.

My cousins understood. They ran off and left me standing under the trees with Toby.

"You had a great idea," I said.

He scuffed the gravel on the path with the toe of his sneaker. "It's funny how much trouble can be avoided if people talk to each other," he said. "I didn't know until today, when I saw the signs, that the location for the Centennial had been changed to the campus."

"Your father didn't tell you?"

He shook his head. "No, but we don't talk much. Actually, I didn't pay much attention to what I'd heard from other people about the Centennial. I'm only in town in the summers and over Christmas, and I won't be going to college here. You probably know more about Fox Crossing than I do."

I didn't say so out loud, but I thought that he probably was right.

"You'll come to the Centennial, though, won't you?" I asked. "It should be lots of fun. My cousins have worked awfully hard on it."

"I know about the clowns," Toby said, laughing. "Thad talks about them all the time. I wouldn't miss seeing them."

"Good," I said.

We stood there awkwardly, not looking at each other.

"Are you part of the clown act?" Toby asked finally.

I shook my head. "Not really. My contribution has been gluing yarn on the ugliest necklace I have ever seen. But yesterday I was part of the parade. A bigger part of it than I'd planned on being." I told him about the wheelbarrow.

"I hope somebody took a snapshot of you," he said.

"No, I don't think so," I said.

"I'd have loved having one."

"Of me in a wheelbarrow with a cast on my leg?"

He looked down at me suddenly, intently. "Of you, no matter what you're riding in or wearing."

"I've got a camera," I said. "We could take pictures of each other. If you wanted to, that is."

"I've got a camera, too. We'll both take pictures. Lots of them."

"When?" I asked. My heart was beating in my throat.

I could see his enthusiasm dying and misery taking its place. "I don't know," he said. "Soon."

I looked down at my feet. "You'll need to sneak away, won't you? To see me, I mean. Is that it?"

He didn't say anything. When I glanced up at him, he was looking straight into my eyes.

"I'll call you when I work something out," he said. "Now I'd better get going."

But he didn't leave.

"What?" I asked.

"Are you okay now?" he asked. "Is your back all right?"

"Pretty much."

"I worried about you a lot."

I nodded. "I'm fine now. Honestly."

"If I had a car, I could take you for a ride," he said. "But I don't. And I guess you shouldn't use a bike now."

"I could, in a while, I think." Ask me! I thought. Make a definite date with me!

"I'll see you," he said.

I watched him go back the way he'd come, jogging a little, probably trying to make up for lost time so his father wouldn't suspect that he'd been talking to any of the terrible Whitney girls.

I got home in time to see Heather and Uncle Will driving away, heading for the college librarian's house. Aunt Marsha greeted me with the news that I had an appointment that afternoon to have my back checked one last time. And, she added, Amelia wasn't coming home for lunch, so the two of us would be eating salad and leftover chicken.

"I like leftovers," I said. "At home in Seattle, we hardly ever have them. Amelia's little brother and sisters eat everything in sight, practically before it's out of the pot."

"Do you like living in a big family?" Aunt Marsha asked.

"Yes. It took getting used to, but now I feel at home there." I set the table in the kitchen for us and poured ice water in our glasses.

We sat down to eat. "I feel sorry for Toby," I said. "He goes away to school, so he doesn't seem to feel at home in Fox Crossing."

"That's not the only reason I feel sorry for Toby," Aunt Marsha said. "It must be hard, growing up with a father like his."

I helped myself to salad. "How did somebody like Mr. Callahan ever get elected mayor?"

Aunt Marsha laughed. "Money. He owns half the town."

"They're rich?" I asked, surprised. Toby didn't act like any of the really rich kids I'd ever known.

Aunt Marsha put down her fork. "I've got an awful hunch that the mayor could win an election again tomorrow, in spite of his bad record. It isn't fair, but people are so impressed with his money that they never stop to think that he doesn't keep his campaign promises."

"Maybe Uncle Will ought to run against him," I said.

Aunt Marsha burst out laughing. "Will the dreamer?" she said. "He'd be eaten alive. No, someday somebody with a thick hide and plenty of money will dump Mayor Callahan. But I hope for Toby's sake that he's not around when it happens."

"Is he mean to Toby?" I asked.

Aunt Marsha scowled. "There's gossip in town that says so."

I shook my head. "Then maybe you're right. For Toby's sake, let's hope nobody takes away the mayor's job too soon."

Later, when Heather came back, I thought about repeating this conversation to her, and then decided against it. Maybe Toby didn't want to be talked about.

Heather was babbling with news anyway. She, Uncle Will, and the librarian were planning on spending the next morning in the college library going through storerooms in the basement. The librarian was sure she'd seen a box of old photographs somewhere.

"Did you take the dinner program to the printer?" I asked.

Heather scowled. "No. Can you believe that Will misplaced it? He said he'd make up another one and take it by himself this afternoon."

"So you've got free time, right?" I asked.

"Yes, so as soon as Amelia gets back, we can change our hair color. If Paige can come over, that is. Why?"

"I have to see the doctor to have my back checked one more time, and I'd like some company," I said. "Could your hair possibly wait?"

"For that reason, certainly," Heather said. "Are you worried?"

"Not really," I said. "But I want to ask him how soon I can go biking again."

"Toby asked you to go on another picnic?" Heather asked. "Good. Just stay away from Lost Lake."

"Well, he didn't exactly ask me," I admitted. "But I think he's going to."

"It's practically the same thing," Heather said.

"I'll twist the doctor's arm a little so you get permission to go. How's that?"

"You're a real romantic, Heather," I said, laughing.

"Hey, what's a cousin for? I'm still in your debt for the greatest parade in Fox Crossing history."

Toby had wanted a snapshot of me in the wheelbarrow. Well, it was too late for that, but not too late for other snapshots. Lots of them, so we can remember each other when the summer is over.

And summer was nearly over.

Chapter 12

Dear Nick: Everything is fine, so stop worrying.
We're going to put on the best Centennial anybody ever saw. And yes, I know when school
starts. Quit nagging me. I'll be home soon, and
we'll hang out at all our favorite places and tell
each other how boring our vacations were.

> It's almost over,
> The older and smarter Erin

All the next day, Heather was in ecstasy. The librarian had found a whole, dusty box full of photographs of the opening celebration for the college, and
she turned it over to Uncle Will and the committee.

Heather bounced out of the den periodically to get
more lemonade, another stack of sandwiches, or another bowl of fruit for the committee. Somebody was
always using the phone, and I gave up hoping that
Toby would call me. The only thing he'd get was a
busy signal.

Aunt Marsha went off after telling me that she had
odds and ends to do at the clinic. I figured she was
getting away from the house before somebody thought
up something for her to do on the committee.

Bear and I stayed on the deck most of the day, both
of us daydreaming in the heat. Amelia came home
once to pick up the horrible necklace that I'd fixed,
and left again, after a quick consultation with the

committee about who did what on which steps a hundred years ago.

"Are you sure you don't want to clown around with us?" she asked me as she headed for the front door, swinging the necklace of shrunken heads as she went.

"My back isn't up to it," I said, trying to sound as pitiful as I could.

"I forgot," she said. "Sorry." And she shut the door behind her, almost catching one head's hair in it.

"They are all demented," I told Bear.

She yawned, making a small, squeaking sound.

"I know, back to the deck," I said.

I heard a burst of laughter from the den as I passed it. The general attitude of the committee had changed since they had found the old photographs.

In the middle of the afternoon, I decided to wander downtown and sort of accidentally drop in at the dress shop where Toby's mother worked. I was curious to see what she was like. She wouldn't know who I was, but maybe, if she seemed extra nice, I'd tell her I was a friend of Toby's.

Then again, maybe that would be a stupid move.

I didn't wear a hat—no point in scaring the lady—and I put on a plain blue skirt and plain white shirt. And ordinary sandals. I looked so average that I hardly recognized myself. But suddenly it seemed safer to me to look as ordinary as possible.

And I carried enough money to actually buy something.

Bear wasn't disappointed being left behind. It was too hot outside for even her.

I walked on the shady sides of the streets, by yards where sprinklers hissed over parched lawns. I seemed to be the only person moving, until I reached the business district. Then the only other human I saw was my aunt, darting into the printer's with a large, brown envelope.

They got her after all, I thought to myself. She's delivering the dinner program, at the last possible moment.

I passed the printer's shop, but my aunt didn't come out, so I continued on. Now that I was getting closer to the dress shop, I began wondering if I'd lost my mind.

What if Toby is there, talking to his mother? Will he think I'm spying?

Why not? I am spying.

Is this such a good idea?

No.

Yes. Keep going, Erin. Maybe you'll learn something about the boy if you meet his mother.

I kept my fingers crossed that somebody else would be in the shop, a customer to keep Mrs. Callahan busy. Maybe, if no one else was there, I'd continue straight down the street to the bookstore. Or the candy store. Even the hardware store.

There was the dress shop. And a woman was walking in! I could have cheered.

I slipped in quietly, after I saw that the woman was talking to someone behind the counter.

Ah, there was a rack of summer dresses, close to the door. I started going through them blindly, not really paying attention to anything. I couldn't see the woman behind the counter clearly, but I knew she had dark hair.

She led the customer to a rack of blouses and took one out. Now I could see Mrs. Callahan clearly.

She was awfully pretty. And she looked much younger than the mayor. Her mouth was like Toby's.

And her hair fell over her forehead the same way his did.

Suddenly she looked up at me and smiled. "I'll be with you in a moment," she said.

Oh, I was stupid to come in here! I couldn't believe I'd done it. Maybe someday Toby would introduce me to her, and she'd remember the girl who'd stood in the shop for ten zillion years gawking at her. Spying on her.

I wanted to run out, but that would have looked even worse. After the customer took the blouse to the back of the shop and disappeared through a door marked "Dressing Rooms," Mrs. Callahan approached me, smiling.

"Can I help you, or are you just browsing?" she asked.

"I'm not sure what I want," I said.

"Go ahead and take your time," she said. "If you have any questions, I'll do my best to help."

And she walked away. No pressure. No hints that I might be wasting her time unless I bought half the store.

I forced myself to stop looking at her and concentrate on the dresses instead. I was holding one that I actually liked, now that I paid attention to it. That was a shock. I seldom bought new clothes, since I'd always been able to find everything I wanted and liked in secondhand stores. The clothing allowance I got from my parents' estate was big enough for me to have closets full of stuff, but I'd never wanted much. Given a choice between new clothes and new art supplies, I'd pick the supplies any day.

Did I have enough money with me to buy this dress? I checked my wallet. Yes, and enough to finance a trip to the candy store, too.

"I'd like to try this on," I told Mrs. Callahan.

"That's one of my favorites," she said when she saw what I was holding up. "Take the dressing room on the right, and call me if you need any help."

I walked past her and went into the dressing room. My hands were shaking.

There was a chair in the cubicle. I sat down until my knees stopped feeling as if they were made of rubber, then I began unbuttoning my shirt. Across the narrow hall, I could hear the other customer muttering something to herself. Finally she called out, "Kathy, can you help me? I've got my hair caught around a button."

I heard Mrs. Callahan come in. Both women laughed. Mrs. Callahan said, "There you go."

Then she rapped on the door of the cubicle where I sat, still scared silly. "Doing all right?"

"Yes," I said.

I got to my feet and made myself change clothes. This was ridiculous. I was acting like a baby.

The dress looked good on me, which surprised me. Ancient, shabby hand-me-downs had always seemed to be my best bets.

Now I ought to do something with my hair, instead of letting it hang in one long braid. Maybe curl it. Maybe cut it.

Maybe lighten it, like my cousins and Paige were planning to do to their hair.

Now I really was losing my mind. I took off the dress and put on my own clothes, then carried the dress out to the counter and told Mrs. Callahan that I'd take it.

"Good," she said. "That's a wonderful color for you. What beautiful hair you have. I remember seeing you a few days back with Paige and some of her friends, and I couldn't help noticing that wonderful,

115

thick braid. Have you moved to Fox Crossing, or are you just visiting?"

"I'm visiting," I said.

I didn't dare tell her I was Heather's cousin. She probably knew how much her husband hated Uncle Will. Right now she seemed to like me. I wanted to keep it that way.

The woman with the blouse came out then and waited behind me, so there was no more time for conversation. I paid for the dress and left the shop.

"Good-bye," Mrs. Callahan called after me.

I turned and looked back at her. All I could manage was a weak smile.

I didn't bother with the candy shop, but went straight home. The committee was breaking up just as I got there. Aunt Marsha was home, slicing cold ham in the kitchen. Amelia and Sandy were sprawled on the deck chairs, drinking iced tea. Sandy wore her Crudella shoes and the horrible necklace.

"All dressed up for a big date tonight?" I asked her, laughing.

"No, but I can tell that you have one," she said. "Let's see what you've got in the sack."

"You went shopping at a real store?" Amelia asked. "I can't believe it. Wait until I tell the kids back in Seattle."

"I saw a dress I liked," I said. "It's not the first time I've been in a dress shop, you know. I've done it before at least twice in my life."

"To laugh at the clothes, I bet," Amelia said. "Or maybe t.p. the dressing rooms."

I scowled at her. "You want to see this dress or sit there making fun of me?"

"Sorry!" she cried. "You know I've actually grown to like what you wear. Let's see the dress. It's probably something I'll want to borrow."

116

Heather joined us then, and the moment she saw the sack, she exclaimed, "You went to see Toby's mother!"

"No, I went to buy a dress," I said. I pulled the dress out of the sack and held it up.

"It's perfect," Amelia said. "I'd borrow it for the Centennial dinner, but I know you're going to wear it."

"Will you tell Toby you got it at his mother's store?" Heather asked.

"I don't even know if I'll be seeing him that night," I said.

Or ever again, I thought.

"He's going," Sandy said. "I heard Thad telling Colin that they'd all be sitting together at the dinner."

I felt my face turn red.

"He won't recognize you," Amelia said, "with a new dress and long blond hair."

"I won't have long blond hair," I said. "And he probably won't recognize me because I'll be behind three bald girls that everybody else will be laughing at."

"What's going on?" Sandy demanded.

They told her and she said, "I'd love to try bleaching my hair."

"You have long, absolutely black hair," I said patiently. "Can you imagine what would happen? It would come out green or purple or something."

"I know," Sandy said, sighing. "That's what happened when I tried it in sixth grade. My hair was the worst color of green. I wore a knit hat for two days until my dad made me take it off so he could see what I'd done to myself. Then the dog barked at me."

"See, Heather? Amelia, are you listening?" I asked. "Bear will have a coronary if you scare her that bad."

"Your stepfather will have a coronary," Sandy advised Heather. "I thought my dad would never stop yelling."

"What did you do about the green color?" I asked. "Heather and Amelia may need to take notes."

"Oh, shut up!" Heather shouted, laughing. She yanked a cushion off a chair and threw it at me, missing me by a mile. "You have no imagination."

"There you're wrong," I said. "I'm an artist."

"Then you may have imagination, but you have no urge to be daring," she retaliated.

"Remember, you are talking to the girl who wears a hat in class," Amelia said.

"If I were you guys, I'd just try bleaching a streak or two, so you can see how it turns out," Sandy told my cousins.

"Right," I said. "Then they can tear it out by the roots if it looks hideous."

"It's going to be all or nothing," Heather declared. "We'll do it the first chance we get, when Paige can be here, too, of course. We'd try it tonight, except that her grandmother's coming over to her house for dinner and she has to be there."

"Why do I feel like the world is about to end?" I asked. "If you do it before the Centennial, all of you are going to wish you had listened to me."

"We want the new look especially for the Centennial," Amelia said.

"Yuck," I said. "Your new look may set the Centennial back a hundred years."

Sandy stayed for dinner, which we ate outside. Once, halfway through dessert, the phone rang, and when Heather ran inside to answer it, I had a dizzy, hopeful feeling that Toby was the one calling, wanting me. But it was Mark Reid, Amelia's boyfriend in Seattle.

She talked to him for a few minutes, then came back out to tell us that he was driving to Fox Crossing for the Centennial, but he might not make it much before dinner. He wanted to know if we knew where he could spend the night.

"You told him he could stay here, I hope," Heather said.

"Was it all right?" Amelia asked Aunt Marsha.

"Certainly," she said. "He can use the couch in the den."

I waited until Uncle Will and Aunt Marsha went inside before I asked Amelia if she was certain she wanted Mark to have a close-up view of her with green hair.

She socked my arm. "He'll love me with blond hair," she said. "I know he will."

"Look, guys," I said, trying to be my most persuasive. "Things are going pretty well right now. You've got a place for the Centennial, the mayor hasn't been able to ruin anything else, the clown act is working out, and nobody is predicting an earthquake or an eruption of Mount St. Helens. Why don't you quit while you're ahead, instead of tempting fate this way?"

They refused to listen to reason, so I gave up on them, went inside, and helped Aunt Marsha with dishes.

"What were you all laughing about out there?" she asked me.

"Trust me, you don't want to know," I said.

"Are we talking about something a parent might worry about?" she asked. I could tell she was concerned.

"No, we're talking about something that a parent might die laughing about," I said.

"Oh, that's all," she said, as she put the last dish in the dishwater.

I stayed up later than usual that night, reading in a corner of the living room. But my mind wasn't on my book. I was still waiting for the phone to ring, wondering where Toby was, wondering if he'd show up at the Centennial after all.

Wondering if we'd ever go biking together again. The doctor said I could. Now would Toby remember to ask me?

No matter how hot the days were, I could tell summer was drawing to a close. Here and there I'd seen red leaves among the green ones on the vine maples. And early in the morning, the air had a hint of autumn in it.

I'd be going home, and Toby would leave for boarding school. Our strange relationship was almost over. But it really hadn't even begun.

Chapter 13

Dear Nick: Thank you for the new (old) hat. Yes, it did cheer me up. You will never know how much we needed it.

Thank you thank you!
Erin

In the morning on the day before the Centennial celebration, Heather and I took Bear for a walk—in the direction of her sister's house, of course. (What other way would she ever let anyone go?)

Heather had cleared it with Thad, to be sure he'd be up and prepared for the invasion. Bear lunged up the walk toward his front porch, whining and wagging her tail, and we could hear Heidi inside yelping as if she'd been stepped on by a dinosaur. Thad opened the door, and Heidi bolted out to greet Bear.

I looked past her, and my heart stopped. Toby stood in the doorway, grinning at me.

"Is that how the two of you say hello when you haven't seen each other for a while?" he asked.

"Not exactly," I said. "Heather is more likely to ask me where I got my hat."

"So where did you get it?" he asked, coming down the steps to join us.

I was wearing a new (old) one that had come in the mail the day before. Good old Nick had been scrounging the used-clothing stores again, and found this one, a wonderful (but somewhat mashed) yellow straw with exactly seventy-six small, dusty daisies around the crown. The hat tied on with wide green ribbons.

"My friend in Seattle sent it," I told Toby.

"It's still got a price tag on it," he said, reaching for the small square of cardboard stapled to the narrow brim.

"Leave it on, please," I said. "I thought that it added a certain flair."

"It says one dollar and thirty-nine cents," Toby said. "When could anybody buy a hat for that?"

"About fifty years ago," I said. "That's why I want the tag left on. It shows that I have traditional values."

"It shows that you are weird," Heather said. "I can stand most of your hats, but that one looks as if something is living in those daisies. Something with more than four legs. I wish you'd stomped on it a few times before you put it on."

Toby laughed and said, "How about you and your hat walking in the opposite direction from the dogs and their friends?"

"Suits me perfectly," I told him. "I don't think I want to take a walk with somebody who doesn't appreciate my appearance."

Heather and Thad went east with the dogs, and Toby and I went west.

"You're not staying at the farm now?" I asked.

"Thad picked me up there late last night," he said. "I'll stay with him until after the Centennial."

I looked up at him. "Not with your parents?"

He shrugged. "Not this time."

I had a strong hunch that his parents didn't even know he was in town.

"What if they see you somewhere? At the Centennial, for instance?" I said, getting straight to the point.

"They won't be going to the celebration," he said. His voice was quiet and steady. He didn't even sound upset. "In fact, my dad is probably already on his way to Seattle. He has business there."

"What about your mother?" I asked.

"She runs a dress shop here," he said. "And she'll probably keep it open. There'll be lots of tourists in the next couple of days. They're always good for her."

I couldn't let him think that I didn't know who his mother was, so I told him that I'd bought a new dress from her the day before, and I'd be wearing it to the Centennial dinner.

He grinned. "I bet you'll look terrific," he said.

"You're going to the dinner, aren't you?" I asked.

"Sure. With Thad's family. We got our tickets weeks ago, before they sold out."

"Toby . . ." I began at the same instant he said, "Erin."

We both laughed.

"You first," he said.

For a long moment, I forgot what I was going to say. I'd never been more nervous. He had to think that I was stupid and ridiculous.

"Do you think it will rain tomorrow?" I asked.

He laughed. "Nope. I think the sun will shine, but it won't be too hot. Now is it my turn to ask you something?"

I nodded.

"Thad will be busy with the clowns tomorrow. In fact, everybody I know will be doing something. So I wondered, well, if you don't have plans, maybe we could spend the day together. You know, walk around and see everything. Have lunch together. Would you like to do that?"

"Sure," I said. I could have jumped and cheered.

"And then," he went on, "after dinner, we could watch the fireworks together."

I was too excited to act cool any longer. "Yes!" I shouted, and I did actually jump up and clap my hands. "Yes!"

My hat bounced crooked in spite of the ribbons that were supposed to hold it in place, so Toby settled it straight on my head again.

"I take it this means you like fireworks," he said.

"It means I like you, too," I blurted.

"Hey," he said. "I'll remember you said that in case you ever get mad at me."

"Why would I get mad at you?"

"Thad says that Heather told him you actually socked a couple of guys." He laughed suddenly. "I can't imagine you losing your temper like that. You're so—so on top of everything."

I shrugged. "There were special circumstances."

"Yeah," he said. "That's what I heard. And I heard that you had the last word."

"And I had the last laugh, too," I added. "Does that bother you?"

"Heck, no," he said. "Some guys need to be set straight. More girls should stick up for themselves."

I looked up at him, grateful that he understood without a lot of explanations. And I was grateful for other reasons, too. "I owe you a lot," I said. "I haven't forgotten that I could have spent the night on that island if it hadn't been for you."

"And I can't forget that you would have been in a hospital a lot sooner if it hadn't been for my father," he said, grim now, the fun gone out of his voice.

"Hey, it worked out all right," I said. "I like canoes."

But he didn't say anything else for a long time, and

124

then he murmured, "I'm really sorry. You can't possibly guess how sorry I am."

I reached out impulsively and grabbed his hand. "It doesn't matter. Here we are, walking down this street together, just the way we're supposed to be."

Neither of us said that being together was probably only temporary.

Everybody was busy that afternoon. Heather and Amelia had dozens of last-minute errands. Uncle Will and Aunt Marsha spent hours with the committee, setting up the college cafeteria for the dinner the next night. I stayed home, answered the phone, and took dozens of messages for everybody.

My cousins and I ate take-out pizza late in the day, around the kitchen table. Uncle Will and Aunt Marsha were going out for a last-minute strategy dinner meeting with the committee. As soon as their car left the driveway, Heather got on the phone and called Paige.

"They're gone," she said. "Come on over, Paige— and don't wear anything that you care about. This is going to be a messy evening."

"I'm trying to believe that I'm having a nightmare," I said when she hung up. "You aren't going to do what I'm afraid you'll do, are you?"

"Tonight's the night we all get a gorgeous new look to dazzle everybody with tomorrow," she said. "Right, Amelia?"

"Right," Amelia said as she dumped the remains of our dinner in the trash can.

"Wrong," I said. "Tonight's the last night you look human. I wish you'd reconsider this plan."

Paige showed up, out of breath and carrying a grocery sack filled with snacks. "I didn't know how long this was going to take, so I came prepared."

"Add it to the pile on the kitchen counter," Amelia said. "We've laid in a few supplies, too."

"You three will end up as fat as pigs and just as bald," I said.

"And you, dear old pal, are a wet blanket with knobs on," Heather said.

Everybody laughed at that. But they didn't change their minds. Heather produced the bottle of peroxide and the box of detergent powder, and they marched into the bathroom. I strolled along behind, with an open bag of potato chips tucked under my arm and a can of pop in one hand. Since there was no way to persuade them to call this experiment off, I decided that I might as well enjoy the spectacle.

It didn't take long before all three of them were gummed up with a mixture of detergent and peroxide. Amelia and Heather sat in the bathtub to "cook." Paige spread out an old towel and sat down cross-legged on the floor. I served snacks and pop.

"Well, now what?" I asked.

"How long will this take?" Heather asked me.

"You should have asked Sandy," I said. "She's the one with experience. I only read about it. I'm afraid you might explode at any time. Your families will see the results on the eleven-o'clock news."

But I didn't worry them. At their request, I timed them by my watch. At ten minutes, I suggested that each of them wash off a lock of hair and see what had happened to it.

"I can tell by looking in the mirror that nothing's happening," Paige said. "Heather, are you sure we've got the right stuff?"

"Yes! It must take longer than ten minutes."

More time ticked by. Amelia couldn't stand it any longer, crawled out of the tub (spilling corn chips in the tub while she was at it), and tried to wipe some of the gook off her hair.

"It's not coming off, Erin," she said.

"Wet a washcloth and try again," I said.

She tried. "It's not working."

"Use more water," I said.

"I'll suds up the whole house," she said.

"Well, how else are we going to get this stuff off?" Heather said.

"Keep trying," I told Amelia.

"I'm going crazy," Heather said, and she crawled out of the tub, too. "What if my hair has turned white instead of blond?"

"Trust me when I tell you that it hasn't," I said. "Look in the mirror. It doesn't look white."

"It looks orange!" Heather yelled.

"It *is* orange!" Paige cried. She jumped up. "So is mine. Look at that. Orange!"

"I think you have to wait longer," I said. "Maybe it turns orange before it turns blond."

"I'm not waiting one more second," Paige said. "Something's gone wrong. I'm taking a shower right this minute."

She stripped off her old T-shirt and shorts, and turned on the water in the tub.

"You're getting the snacks all wet!" Amelia cried.

"I don't care!" Paige said.

"Come on, let's go upstairs and shower off there," Heather told Amelia. "I'll take Mom's bathroom. You use the other."

I followed them. Bear followed me, licking up potato chip crumbs. While the showers upstairs ran, I strolled back and forth shouting encouragement. And laughing.

"You just shut up!" Amelia yelled at me.

127

Finally all the showers shut off. I didn't hear a sound.

I stood at the head of the stairs and sang that corny song somebody always sings at the Miss America contests.

"Erin, shut up!" everybody yelled.

"Come on out, ladies," I called. "Let's see the beautiful blondes."

Paige came out first. She stood at the foot of the steps, wrapped in a towel. Her hair was as orange as a carrot.

"I wish I was dead," she said.

Behind me, Amelia and Heather straggled down the hall. Both of them wore bathrobes. Both of them had hair that was part orange, part brown. And part pale blond.

"Well," I said helpfully, "at least two of you almost got it right."

Long before Uncle Will and Aunt Marsha came home, I'd cleaned up all three bathrooms. Paige went home as soon as she was certain that her parents were watching TV in their bedroom and wouldn't see her as she came in. My cousins got into their pajamas and went to bed. Blow-dried, their hair looked even worse than it had before. I refused Amelia's offer of everything she owned in exchange for the bottom twelve inches of my hair.

"I'll glue it on my head with that stuff Will uses to mend broken stuff," she said.

"I'll lend you one of my hats instead," I said.

"Which one?"

"The daisy hat," I said.

"But that hat is the worst one you have," she said.

"Yes. And it's perfect for Mindy Brunch, the fat

lady. Now go to sleep. It's midnight. Tomorrow's the big day.''

"By tomorrow morning, I should be a thousand miles away by broomstick," Amelia said. "Nobody will ever find me. Why did I do this to myself, Erin?"

"You and Heather seem to have an urge to self-destruct," I said. "The two of you now look so horrible that I think somebody should step on you and squash you before you decide to reproduce. The world already has too many problems."

"Oh, thank you," she said bitterly as she reached out for her bedside lamp and turned it out. "Good night. I hope you have nightmares."

"Sleeping next to you? It's guaranteed. Good night, cousin. Just think—it could be worse."

"How?" she groaned miserably.

"Think how you'd feel if you were Heather and weren't going to be a clown tomorrow. You at least have an excuse for looking weird. What's she going to do?"

"She could wear your green velvet hat," Amelia said. "When you wear it, you look like you're hiding under a mildewed toadstool. She couldn't possibly look any worse."

I sat up in bed and stared across the room at her. "Was that some sort of shot?"

"You'd better believe it," she said. "And I've got a lot more where that came from. Now be quiet and let me sleep."

I snickered as I lay down again. "I'd sleep if I could, but your hair glows in the dark."

"Cousin," Heather hissed, "trust me when I tell you to quit while you're ahead."

That night I dreamed first of bike-riding along country roads with Toby, always ending up where we started, never getting anywhere. And then I dreamed of riding alone, down a long road toward Seattle. I kept looking back, but there was never anybody else in sight. Not ever.

Chapter 14

Dear Nick: Here's an official postcard for the Fox Crossing College Centennial. It's nearly over.

Ready to drop,
Erin

In the morning, my cousins spent a half hour trying on my hats before they had enough courage to go downstairs. Amelia, desperate to draw attention away from her bizarre hair, had even put on part of her clown makeup.

"Try this again," I said, handing her the daisy hat for the tenth time. "It is best with your costume. All those fussy little flowers go perfectly with the fussy pattern in your curtains."

She jammed the hat down over her head again and glared at me from under the brim. "My hair still shows."

"Push it up underneath. Pin it in place."

"Erin, you think you have the answer for everything," she snarled. "Just wait. Someday you'll want to look terrific, and I won't help you a bit."

"If you think that you look terrific in that fat dress, you are out of your mind," Heather said crossly. "Both of us look ridiculous, and that's that."

She was wearing my green velvet hat, so I reached over and turned the brim down all the way around. "Now your hair hardly shows," I said.

"And neither does my face," she said. "I look as if I was hiding from the police. What will Mom think when she sees me?"

"You could try telling the truth," I said. "I've found that it usually solves the problem."

"Yes, and you've spent more time in the guidance counselor's office than anybody else in our high school," Amelia grouched. "So much for naked truth."

"Aunt Marsha may even have an idea about covering up the damage," I argued. "Give her a chance."

"If I thought there was a chance of getting past her lecture and straight on to the help, I'd say we should tell Mom," Heather said. "As it is, I'm sure we'd be sorry."

"You two are making a big deal out of this, and it's stupid," I said. "Why don't I go down and tell her that you've run into a little problem and would appreciate her help, but your nerves aren't up to any adult opinions this morning?"

Both of them stared at me. "Have you gone completely insane?" Heather asked. "Can you imagine a grown-up passing by an opportunity to give an opinion?"

I'd finished dressing in white shorts and a red shirt, so I plopped on my neat little hat with the rose over my own plain brown hair and started for the door. "Okay, suit yourselves. I'll keep your secret, but I'm hungry and I don't want to sit up here with the two of you for the rest of the day while you have hysterics. Amelia, the clowns are supposed to meet you . . ."

"I know, I know," Amelia cried. "You are the biggest nag I ever knew! I'll wear the nasty daisy hat—I know there's a spider living in it!—and go. But if you laugh, I'll do something to you that hurts."

132

"I won't laugh anymore," I said. "I lay awake half the night laughing, and I'm all worn-out."

And with that big lie, I marched out of the room and downstairs.

"What's keeping the rest of the crowd?" Uncle Will asked when I sat down at the breakfast table.

"They're dressing," I said.

"It sounds as if World War Three was beginning," he said. "Here, have a slice of melon. I can spoon a little yogurt over it, if you like."

"Yuck," I said.

"I admire your taste," Will said, as he passed the fruit platter to me.

Aunt Marsha poured juice for me. "Is Amelia excited?" she asked. "We're looking forward to seeing her clown act."

"She's already got part of her makeup on," I said. "She loves being a clown."

Uncle Will looked at his watch. "Heather tells me that the first vendors start around the Quad at ten-thirty, and the different acts are scheduled to begin at the same time. Are you planning on being there?"

I nodded, my mouth full.

"You can walk around with us, if you like," Aunt Marsha said.

"I made plans, but thanks anyway." I didn't dare look up.

"Oh, is Toby in town?" Aunt Marsha asked.

"Yes."

"Well, his father isn't," Uncle Will said. "Enjoy yourself."

I grinned. "While the cat's away," I said.

"That's a big, mean cat," Aunt Marsha said. "You'd better be careful."

I took a sip of juice. "Maybe I owe him one. He's the one who had better look out."

Uncle Will shouted with laughter, but Aunt Marsha looked worried. "I know you're spunky," she began.

"Hey," I said, "I don't have a thing to lose. I'm leaving town anyway. What's he going to do, give me a bad grade in geometry?"

My cousins came in then, looking guilty as well as peculiar.

"Ah, Heather," Uncle Will said when he saw his stepdaughter. "I see you borrowed one of Erin's hats."

"Yes," she said brightly. "Where's my yogurt?"

"It's phoning home," Uncle Will said soberly, "and it said you shouldn't wait for it to get to the table."

"Stop that!" Heather cried. She helped herself to the fruit platter and grabbed two pieces of toast.

Amelia slid into her seat and picked up her juice glass. She wouldn't look anybody in the eye.

"That's wonderful makeup," Aunt Marsha said. "I like the way you draw on those long eyelashes. Everybody will love you."

"I'm glad," Amelia said. Then she changed the subject quickly. "Do you think it's going to be hot today?"

"Afraid so," Uncle Will said. "Maybe not as hot as yesterday, but you're going to feel it."

Just then, somebody rang the front doorbell. Aunt Marsha answered it, and came back leading Paige, dressed up as the spoiled little girl, Pansy. She was wearing a wig made out of orange yarn, and it hid her orange hair fairly well.

"Better hurry, Amelia," she said. "Rod needs your help. Some of the cotton came out of his stuffed gorilla, and Mom's trying to sew up the hole right now, but it's not going to look right."

"How did the cotton come out?" Amelia demanded.

"Rod got into his Lionrump costume last night, turned on that stupid noise tape in his helmet, and was dragging the gorilla around town so everybody could have a preview, and a dog on Primrose Street bit it. Come on, let's go. You can eat later. This is an emergency."

Amelia rushed upstairs to put on the rest of her costume while Paige waited in the hall.

I sidled up to her and whispered, "Is the gorilla really losing its insides, or is that a way of getting Amelia out of the house before somebody realizes that that mess is really her hair?"

"The gorilla is missing a large part of its behind," Paige said. "Honestly. I could have killed Rod when I found out. It took us days and days to stuff that gorilla costume, and then he goes and spoils it because he can't quit showing off."

Amelia thundered downstairs, dressed as Mindy Brunch. "Okay, we're off," she said. "Tell Heather I'll be waiting for her signal to begin the act."

I would have passed along the message, but Heather heard it herself as she bolted past us on her way upstairs. "Gotta go," she said. "I have a meeting with the girls who are acting as guides in the park, in case anybody misses the signs."

She paused once and looked down at us. "Do I look dumb?"

"Only odd," Amelia said. "Nobody's going to care."

"When Thad sees me, he'll stop speaking to me," she said, despairing.

"He'll be too busy with the clowns," Amelia said. "You won't have to explain anything until tonight, at the dinner."

135

"By that time, maybe I'll be lucky enough to be dead," Heather said, and she ran the rest of the way up the stairs to finish dressing.

Five minutes later, she was gone, too. I went back to the kitchen and took another slice of melon. "When are you people leaving?" I asked.

"Not for a while yet," Aunt Marsha said. "Erin, tell me the truth. What did those girls do to their hair?"

I considered my answer carefully. "They wanted to look beautiful for the Centennial, but they made a slight miscalculation last night."

"I wish they'd said something when we got home," Aunt Marsha said. "I'd have covered the mess up with a temporary rinse. I've got some, and it would have done until I had a chance to get them to a hairdresser for a decent repair."

"You have some of this temporary rinse?" Uncle Will asked curiously. "You color your hair?"

"Oh, mind your own business!" Aunt Marsha said.

I left while Uncle Will was still laughing.

Toby was waiting for me in the park. "You're right on time," he said.

"I'm always on time," I told him. "We've got fifteen minutes before things start happening. What do you want to do until then?"

He looked around at the crowd of people streaming through the park, following signs toward the campus. "We'd better find ourselves a good place to watch the fun. The Quad's going to be jammed. Just like it was a hundred years ago."

He was responsible for pointing Heather and Uncle Will in the direction of old photographs, so he was responsible for what we saw ahead of us on the campus—vendors dressed in old-fashioned clothes, pushing carts with wide, striped umbrellas. The steps of the Quad buildings were decorated with banners and streamers, as they had been so long ago. If his father ever found out Toby's part in this, what would he do?

I pushed the worry away. "Look," I said, "there are the clowns. Hey, they've got the bagpipe player with them!"

We hurried to catch up to the marching clowns, and found a place under a tree not too far from the steps of the Engineering Building, where they planned to put on their act. Both of us had brought cameras, so we took pictures of each other and everything else around us. After a while, a lemonade vendor passed us, close enough for Toby to call out an order to him.

We watched and listened, sipping lemonade, while the crowds grew thicker.

"This will be a big success," Toby said. "All of it, I'll bet. Come on, let's wander around the Quad and see what else is going on."

We left the clowns and circled around to see the folk dancers. I recognized some of them—they'd been at the dance where I met Toby.

I treated us to sausage rolls from another vendor, and then we moved to the steps where a barbershop quartet sang.

Twice we passed Aunt Marsha and Uncle Will. Twice Uncle Will winked at me. But Aunt Marsha seemed worried.

"I don't think your aunt likes me," Toby said.

"It's not you," I said.

"Maybe."

"It doesn't really have anything to do with us, you know," I said.

"My dad involved you," he said.

"That's over with," I told him, trying to reassure him. But I didn't really mean it. The more I thought about Mr. Callahan, the angrier I got. But it wouldn't do to let Toby know about it.

By midafternoon, we'd seen all the entertainment and we'd eaten enough to last us for a week. We started going through the buildings on the campus then, looking at the exhibits.

"Would you like to go to this college?" I asked Toby.

"No," he said. "It's too close to home."

How awful, I thought. I couldn't imagine wanting to go away to college just to get away from my family.

"What about you?" he asked. "Have you made any plans for after high school?"

I shook my head. "I have trouble making plans for next month," I said.

He laughed. "I wish I could be more like you."

"Try it," I said. "You'll like it."

"Maybe I'll have to settle for watching you."

I liked the sound of that, but I couldn't see that we had much of a future together, not after this summer. But I didn't say it aloud. I didn't even want to think about it.

At six, Toby walked me home and promised to meet me at seven for the Centennial dinner. Aunt Marsha and Uncle Will were already there, changing clothes.

"Are Heather and Amelia here?" I asked.

"No, and I'm wondering if I ought to go out looking for them," Aunt Marsha said. "If I hurried, I think I could fix their hair before we have to show up at the dinner."

"With your pot of hair dye," Uncle Will said. He was putting on his tie in front of the hall mirror, and I saw him grin at himself.

Aunt Marsha looked at him with narrow eyes. "If

you knew what I really look like, you wouldn't have married me. So be careful what you tease me about. I may decide to be myself one of these days, and scare you right out from under what's left of your hair."

Uncle Will kept grinning. "Listen to her, Erin. Scary, right?"

"I make a point of not getting involved in this sort of family discussion," I said, and I went into the room I shared with Amelia and shut the door.

My new dress was hanging on the back of the closet door, freshly pressed. I dug through my sack of shoes, found sandals that looked good enough to be seen in public, and laid out a long ribbon I planned to braid with my hair.

I had showered, dressed, and was braiding my hair when Amelia crept into my room, still wearing her fat costume.

"Are Aunt Marsha and Uncle Will still here?" she whispered.

"Sure," I said. "Where have you been?"

"At the drugstore," she said. She pulled a sack out from under her billowing dress. "See? It's one of those temporary rinses. The lady in the drugstore said it might cover up the mess I made of my hair, or maybe it wouldn't, but it would be worth a try. Heather's got one, too, and so does Paige."

"Aunt Marsha knew this morning what you'd done," I said. "She was going to put a rinse on your hair. You wasted your money."

"She knows?" Amelia cried. "Is she going to kill us?"

"I think she looks at your day of humiliation as enough punishment. But what's Mark going to say when he gets here? You didn't forget about him, did you?"

"Of course I didn't forget," Amelia said. She wig-

139

gled out of her costume and left it in a heap on the floor. "He'll be here any minute, so you go downstairs and tell him I'm taking a long shower and I'll be with him as soon as I can."

I looked at my watch. "You haven't got much time before the dinner starts," I said.

"Oh, who cares!" she said. "I can miss the dinner if I have to. I just don't want to scare Mark to death."

I thought that it was more likely he'd laugh himself to death, but I didn't say that out loud. "Okay, I'll go down and wait for him," I said. "But you might end up still needing a hat."

"I hope not," she said fervently.

I walked across the hall and knocked on Heather's door. She stuck her head out just long enough to ask if either one of the bathrooms was free. She was still wearing the green hat.

"Both bathrooms are empty, but Amelia's going to put that stuff on her hair—"

"Hush!" Heather said. "Mom will hear you and want to know what's going on."

"She already knows." I repeated her mother's invitation to her, and Heather turned pale.

"Was she mad?"

"Nope," I said. "She thinks you're an idiot, though."

"Oh, well," Heather said, "what's new about that?"

"You know that this rinse probably won't cover up all the damage," I volunteered.

"Thanks, you supportive old pal," Heather said. "If ever I need somebody to tell me how ugly and stupid I am, I'll call you." And she banged the door.

I would have said, "I told you so," but I restrained myself and went downstairs to wait for Mark.

He showed up ten minutes later, apologizing for

being a little later than he'd planned, but traffic, he said, was awful.

"Where's Amelia?" he asked.

"Getting ready," I said.

"I wish I could have been here to see her clown act. Was she good?"

"Perfect, as always," I said. "But she didn't get much help from this guy with the stuffed gorilla."

"I heard about him," Mark said. "I wonder if he's willing to part with the gorilla. I think we could use him as a regular part of our act in Seattle."

"I doubt that," I said. "The clowns are keeping their act, even after Amelia leaves. They've already had offers to work at a couple of parties and the county fair. Anyway, the gorilla's missing part of his rear end." I explained about the dog.

Mark was still laughing when Amelia came down the stairs. For a moment, I know she thought that he was laughing at her, so I jumped in and said, "Gee, you look great."

She did, except for her hair, which was now a sort of dull brown. She had curled it up more than she usually did, so if someone wasn't expecting the color difference, it might seem as if the only change was the curls.

"I'm sure glad to see you," Mark told her. "I wish I could have been here earlier. Erin says the clown act was great."

"It was," Amelia said. "The best part is that they've decided to keep on with the act. Now I feel like all the time I spent with them was worth it." She plucked at her hair nervously. "Maybe we should get started."

Uncle Will and Aunt Marsha came down then, with Heather creeping along behind. She was still wearing the green hat, so I had to conclude that the rinse hadn't worked too well on her.

Amelia introduced Mark to them, and we started off on foot toward the college when Uncle Will assured us that we wouldn't find a parking place anywhere near it.

At exactly seven, we arrived. Toby and Thad were waiting together outside the door. We separated after we got inside, Uncle Will and Aunt Marsha heading toward the speakers' table, and the rest of us toward our reserved places in the nearest table.

"You look nice," I told Toby. He was wearing a sport jacket and slacks instead of his usual jeans.

"You look better than nice," he said. "I brought you this." He pulled a pink rose out of his pocket and handed it to me.

"From the farm?" I asked.

"I brought it in with me yesterday," he said, "and kept it in water. It's one of the last."

One of the last. For a moment, my eyes stung with tears. But then a man got up and began a speech about the college, so I blinked and smiled.

Then it was Uncle Will's turn to make a speech. He didn't say much about the college—most of his speech was about someone who had helped the Centennial committee plan the celebration, someone who had unselfishly given time and energy without complaint, someone who deserved the plaque he was holding in his hands.

"This," he said, "is for my daughter, Heather."

Heather burst into tears, and the rest of us jumped to our feet and clapped.

She grabbed me. "I can't go up there and accept it," she whispered. "I look like a dork."

"A very special dork," I said. "Get going, or I'll grab back my hat."

Thad led her to the speakers' table and stood back. Uncle Will handed her the plaque and kissed her cheek.

For the first time, I took a good long look at the program, and I understood why Aunt Marsha and Uncle Will had gone to so much trouble to keep Heather from seeing it. Her name was printed there, as the recipient of the plaque.

I was filled to the brim with satisfaction. All the Whitney girls had started out with problems, and two of us had solved them. Amelia had started a clown troupe in Fox Crossing, and Heather was the star of the Centennial.

All that was left was me—and there was no way of solving my problem.

Chapter 15

Dear Nick: Ready or not, here I come.

Glad/Sorry to be heading home,
Erin

Late that night, when the Centennial celebration was over, and the last of the fireworks sputtered out above us, Toby and I walked back through the campus together and met our friends on the sidewalk outside the gates.

Heather was still clutching her plaque as if it would disappear if she let go of it for even a second.

Amelia, trailed by Mark and the Fox Crossing branch of her clown troupe, hurried up and asked us if we were interested in following Sandy home and putting together a late meal.

"Count me in," Thad said.

"I'm starved," Toby said. "Practically hungry enough to eat Erin's hat."

"Then let's go," Amelia said. "I saw Aunt Marsha and Uncle Will a couple of minutes ago, and they said it was all right, as long as we don't stay out too late."

"Then forward, march," Rod shouted. He was still in his Lionrump costume, dragging the poor gorilla behind him in a wagon.

We made quite a parade, winding our way through people hurrying to find their cars, and others walking this way and that to the various dormitories and rooming houses that were putting up the old graduates.

Sandy's parents were already home when we got there, and they had started cooking hamburgers.

I put a new roll of film in my camera and started taking pictures. Naturally I did my best to get Toby in practically every shot. I'd need the pictures in the days and months to come.

I hadn't had the courage yet to ask him if he'd write to me after he went away to boarding school. I wasn't even certain if it was such a good idea. Maybe letters would make things worse.

Maybe I was exaggerating everything in my mind.

By the time everybody had finished eating, some of us were feeling the effects of the long day. Even Rod, who seemed to have endless ideas for aggravating everybody with his gorilla, yawned a few times.

"We'd better go," Amelia said. "Mark's exhausted, and so am I."

"Toby and I will walk you cousins home," Thad said.

We thanked Sandy's parents for the great meal and one by one straggled out on the porch. The clowns, with Rod pulling his gorilla (which was now holding an empty potato chip sack against its chest and wearing somebody's cowboy hat), went in one direction, and my cousins and I, with the boys, went in another.

When we got out of reach of the racket the clowns were raising, Heather said, "I'm glad I won't be around for the bicentennial. I couldn't go through all this again."

"What? You don't want another award?" Thad asked.

She hugged her plaque a little closer. "Not if I have to work that hard to get it. I wish everybody on the committee had been given one, though. They did just as much work as I did.''

''No way,'' Amelia said. ''You were all over town all the time.''

''The best part was the way Will introduced me,'' Heather said. She was quiet for a moment, then cleared her throat. ''He called me his daughter, not his stepdaughter.''

''I heard that,'' I said.

''Me, too,'' Amelia said. ''Good for you.''

We arrived at our front porch. Toby took my hand and said, ''Do you want to go biking on the day after tomorrow? Are you up to it?''

''I'm fine, honestly,'' I said. ''Where will we go this time?''

''I thought you might like to see the island from the side of the lake where the farm is.''

''Will you show me the wind chimes?'' I asked.

''I'll let you start the birds singing,'' he said. ''There won't be many more chances. They'll be flying south soon.''

Soon. Autumn was coming. It was almost here.

''See you the day after tomorrow,'' I said.

''At ten sharp,'' he said. ''I'll bring lunch again.''

I waved good-bye from the doorway. My cousins and Mark followed me in. We were too tired to talk much. Mark's bed had been made up for him on the couch in the den, so we all said good night to him and went upstairs.

Aunt Marsha met us in the hall. ''Everybody still got hair?'' she asked. ''I took the time to make appointments for Heather and Amelia tomorrow morning with my hairdresser. She said she might be able to hide your big adventure.''

''Was she laughing?'' Heather demanded.

''Naturally,'' Aunt Marsha said. ''She told me that

she'd done the same thing when she was your age. Most girls try something like that."

"Did you?" I asked. I couldn't help grinning.

"Do you think I'd admit something like that at a time like this?" Aunt Martha said.

Uncle Will popped his head out the bedroom door. "Hey, lady," he said to Aunt Marsha. "What color is your hair, anyway?"

"The color yours used to be when you still had hair," Aunt Marsha said, and she marched past him, her nose in the air.

"Good night, group," Uncle Will said to us.

Heather pulled off the green hat and handed it to me. "Thanks, Erin. I don't know if I'll be able to live down this hat, but I'll try."

"Hey," I said, as I smoothed the velvet under my fingers. "You could have gone out into the world just as you are. And then tried living that down."

Bear thundered upstairs and jumped up on Heather's bed. Amelia and I took the hint and shut our door.

"Are you glad it's over?" I asked.

"Oh, glad," she said, with a big sigh. She pulled off the daisy hat and stared at herself in the mirror over the dresser. "I look like an explosion."

"You look like cafeteria food," I said.

"Go to bed, Erin," she said. "And when we get back to Seattle, don't you dare tell anybody about this."

"Who would believe me?" I asked.

Two days later, Toby and I biked out to the farm, and he showed me the old wind chimes hanging in a tree.

"Let's have our picnic here," I said. "Then, for dessert, I'll start the birds singing."

147

We spread a bright red blanket under the trees and set out our lunch. The hired man came by after a while, offering us icy water from the well.

"When do you leave for school?" he asked Toby.

"In ten days," Toby told him.

Ten days. I'd be gone by then. Amelia and I were returning to Seattle Friday morning.

"Will you be staying out here at the farm until then?" the hired man asked Toby.

"Until the last day," Toby said.

"Good," the man said, and he left us alone.

"You'll be glad to leave town, won't you?" I asked Toby.

He nodded. "I'm always glad to leave."

"Do you miss your mother?" I asked.

He nodded again. "But we call each other every week."

We finished our sandwiches in silence. Then, without thinking it through, I blurted, "It must be hard, not getting along with your father. But it's hard not having a father. Sometimes I would have settled for a mean dad, just so I could have had one."

"Some things can't be fixed," he said. He looked off into the distance, where the lake glittered in the sun. "When too much has happened for too long, people quit caring."

"So what's going to happen to you now?" I asked.

"I'll finish high school, and then go on to college, and then, someday, if I'm lucky, I'll be able to come back to the farm."

I crumpled up my sandwich wrappings and shoved them back in the basket. I couldn't think of anything more to say.

"Is it time for dessert?" Toby asked.

I looked up and saw his smile, and I couldn't help smiling, too. "Here comes dessert," I said.

I got up and reached out to the wind chimes, dragging my fingers across the glass pieces slowly, over and over, until the birds on the island sang out their answer.

"I'll remember this for the rest of my life," I said.

"Here's something I'll remember for the rest of my life," Toby said, and he pulled out his wallet. "I got my rolls of film developed yesterday. Look at this."

He had two pictures of me in his wallet. In one, I was laughing into the camera, holding my hat on with one hand. I remembered when he took it.

But I hadn't known that he'd taken the other one. It showed me in the distance, standing under a tree.

"I look so lonely in this one," I said.

"I thought you looked more like you were waiting for something. Or someone."

I looked closer at the picture. "I guess I was waiting for you," I said.

He took the wallet and put it back in his pocket. "I know you won't. Keep waiting, that is. I don't know when I'll see you again, or even if I ever will. But I'll look at that picture a lot, and think about the time when you really were waiting for me."

"We could write," I said. "Would you answer me if I sent you a letter?"

"Sure," he said. "I'd like to get mail from you."

We stood looking at each other for a long time. "This is all so stupid," I said. "If you went to school in Fox Crossing, then I'd see you every once in a while."

He sighed and glanced away. "Maybe some night you'll see the stars and think about the time I brought you back from the island."

"Yes," I said.

He looked down at me again. "I've never even kissed you," he said.

"No," I said. "I guess you'd better. Right now."

On our last day in Fox Crossing, Amelia and I went around saying good-bye to the friends we'd made. We spent half the day visiting, and were walking home through the park when we saw Mayor Callahan coming toward us. The only way he could avoid us was to turn out on the grass, and he wasn't about to do that.

"Oh, boy," Heather murmured. "I hate this."

"Listen, you go on home," I said quickly. "I've got something I want to say to him."

"Stomp on him," Heather advised.

She dodged around him and trotted away, and I blocked his path.

"I love telling people how you left me on the island when you knew I was hurt," I said. "If you think I'm going to let anybody forget what happened, you're crazy."

He was going to brush past me, but I blocked him again.

"You never know, when you pass people on the street, if they're laughing at you or despising you," I went on. "But there is one thing you do know. I bet you've already figured out that someday you won't have anybody around who cares what happens to you. And then you'll have a turn on an island, or someplace else where you'll be all alone. All alone and nobody will help. When it happens, remember that I told you it would."

He stepped out on the grass to get around me.

"Hey!" I yelled at his back. "When people pass you, try to guess if they're laughing at you or not."

He hurried a little faster. The back of his neck was red.

I settled my hat on my head and started home. Good for you, Erin, I told myself. You always know where to poke a sharp stick.

Amelia and I thought we'd seen the last of the clowns, but the next morning when we arrived at the bus station, the whole troupe showed up, in costume. Even the man who played the bagpipes was there, tootling away. It was probably the biggest send-off anybody ever got in Fox Crossing.

Toby and I didn't have any time alone. But after I got on the bus and sat by a window, he reached up one hand and pressed it against the glass, and I pressed mine against the same spot.

"Remember me," I whispered.

He read my lips and nodded his head.

The bus started up, the bagpipes let out an earsplitting honk, and we were on our way.

"This was some vacation," Amelia said. "I'm so worn-out that I need another vacation to recover."

"School starts next week," I said. The bus was passing trees that already bore a few red and gold leaves.

"We don't even have school clothes yet," Amelia said.

"I'm in pretty good shape," I said. "I'll just recycle last year's stuff, and maybe look for a new jacket at First Pick."

It was hard for me to concentrate on a conversation about clothes. I had left Toby behind. All I could think about was the last sight I'd had of him, waving good-bye.

Amelia fell asleep after a while, but I watched out the window, wondering what my future would be like.

I'd never given it much thought before. Sooner or later I'd have to decide what I wanted to do to take care of myself when I was out of school. I'd have to make plans.

Toby had made plans for himself. Eventually he'd return to Fox Crossing and the farm.

Would I ever again hear the birds singing to the glass harp?

Amelia woke up when the bus reached Seattle. "Did I miss anything?" she asked.

"Nothing much," I said. "The bus driver stopped first to throw off a man who inflated an air mattress in the aisle. Then he stopped to let off a woman who'd smuggled a chicken on board."

"You're making this up," Amelia said as she yanked a comb through her dark blond hair.

"I most certainly am not making it up," I said. "The chicken's name was Claudia. Would I make up something like that?"

"Who knows what you'd do," Amelia said. "Do I look all right? Is Mom going to take one look at me and accuse me of trying to bleach my hair?"

"Probably," I said. "I expect Aunt Marsha phoned her as soon as the bus left Fox Crossing to tell her the whole sordid story."

Amelia slumped in her seat. "Oh, well. It could have been worse."

Nothing could have been worse for me than what happened, I thought. I met somebody I never dreamed I'd meet, and I might never see him again. And if I didn't, remembering him would hurt me so much that I didn't think I could stand it.

The bus pulled into the station, and the driver opened the door. Through the window, I saw Aunt Ellen and Uncle Jock, all the little guys, and my old pal, Nicholas Brown. It was a sunny day, but Nick was holding up an orange umbrella missing at least a third of its slats.

"We're home," Amelia said.

Home, I thought. I climbed off the bus, hugged my family, and shook hands with Nick.

"Now will you please tell me everything that happened to you in Fox Crossing?" Nick demanded. "I've waited long enough."

"I had a picnic, went to the Centennial celebration, and said good-bye," I told him. "Hey, where'd you get that great umbrella?"

"It's for you," Nick said proudly. "I bought it from a guy in the alley behind that big fish store near the waterfront."

He passed the umbrella to me, and I held it over my head.

"Perfect," I said. "Nick, you are priceless."

"Hey," he said. "We try."

I folded the umbrella and piled into the van with my family. Nick, who was on his way to a used bookstore, faded into the crowd on the sidewalk.

As we headed home, I looked north. Farther away than I could see, but not out of reach of my imagination, wind chimes sang and hundreds of starlings responded, a last song before they left the island.

Summer was over.

JEAN THESMAN is the author of many books for young people, including *The Rain Catchers*. She lives in Washington state with her husband and several dogs.

Avon Flare Presents
THE WHITNEY COUSINS
by Award-Winning Author
JEAN THESMAN

*Three teenage girls dealing with
the complexity of growing up—*

HEATHER   75869-5/$2.95 US/$3.50 Can
For Heather, adjusting to a new stepfamily and new town is
tough, especially at fifteen. But when her new stepsister's hon-
esty is questioned, threatening her chances for a scholarship,
Heather pulls for her, learning what it means to be a family.

AMELIA   75874-1/$2.95 US/$3.50 Can
When Warren, a handsome senior, takes Amelia out and tries
to force her to go too far, Amelia is afraid to tell anyone
because they might think she was "asking for it."

ERIN   75875-X/$2.95 US/$3.50 Can
Erin Whitney's parents were killed by a drunk driver when she
was ten, and she's been shuffled from relative to relative ever
since. But the Whitneys are a tough bunch and can see
through to Erin's pain—making her feel, at last, that she has a
real home.

TRIPLE TROUBLE   76464-4/$3.50 US/$4.25 Can
Amelia and Erin are staying with Heather for a summer of fun,
adventure...and romance!

FLARE NOVELS BY
Ellen Emerson White

FRIENDS FOR LIFE 82578-3/$2.95 U.S./$3.50 Can.
A heart-wrenching mystery about Susan McAllister, a
high school senior whose best friend dies—supposedly
of a drug overdose. Her efforts to clear her friend's
reputation and identify the killer bring her closer to the
truth—and danger.

THE PRESIDENT'S DAUGHTER
88740-1/$2.95 U.S./$3.50 Can.
When Meg's mother runs for President—and wins—
Meg's life becomes anything but ordinary.

ROMANCE IS A WONDERFUL THING
83907-5/$2.95 U.S./$3.50 Can.
Trish Masters, honor student and all-around preppy, falls
in love with Colin McNamara—the class clown. As their
relationship grows, Trish realizes that if she can give Colin
the confidence to show his true self to the world, their
romance *can* be a wonderful thing.

WHITE HOUSE AUTUMN
89780-6/$2.95 U.S./$3.25 Can.
In the sequel to THE PRESIDENT'S DAUGHTER,
Meg struggles to lead a normal life as the daughter of the
first woman President of the United States.